Wee Folk

and Wise

Edited by Deby Fredericks

WolfSinger Publications ❧ Brackettville, Texas

Acknowledgments

"Beware the Fairy's Price" © Lillian Csernica
"Children in the Sky" © Michael Lee Johnson
"Offering" © Kara Race-Moore
"Under the Roses" © Elizabeth Guizzetti
"The Farmer and the Fairy" © James Penha.
Originally published in *Verve* (1998)
"The Dullahan's Coach" © Samuel Poots
"Gog From Magog © Matthew A Timmins
"The Fiddler" © H. A. Titus
"Pixie Crystals" © Phyllis Irene Radford
"The Ties That Bind" © Sarah Joy Adams
"Over Coffee" © Teresa Milbrodt
"Dances With Elves" © Cynthia Ward.
Originally published in *Galaxy Magazine* (1995).
"The Magic in the Melody" © Shayna Coplan
"Silver and Scythe" © Manny Frishberg and Edd Vick
"The Last Son of Auberon" © Ben Stewart
"Inked Out" © Brandy T. Wilson
"Dandelion" © Deby Fredericks

Copyright © 2024 by WolfSinger Publications
Individual Stories copyrighted to their authors.

1st published by SkyWarrior Book Publishing 2017

2nd Edition
Published by WolfSinger Publications
All rights reserved.

For permission requests, please contact WolfSinger Publications at:
editor@wolfsingerpubs.com

This novel is a work of fiction. names, characters, places and incidents are either the product of the authors imaginations, or, if real, used fictitiously.

No generative AI was used in the conceptualization, development, or drafting of the individual stories presented here. Cover creation as noted below.

Cover Art created by Carol Hightshoe using Midjourney Generative AI and stock photos.

ISBN 978-1-944637-57-6

Bound and printed in the United States

Editor's Note

Back in 2015, I approached my good friend, Maggie Bonham of Sky Warrior Books, about putting together an anthology of fairy stories. She said yes, and so the anthology *Wee Folk and Wise* was created.

Time flew like a fairy, and the anthology went out of print. Then a new publisher, Carol Hightshoe of Wolfsinger Publications, acquired some of Sky Warrior's catalog. This included reissuing my fantasy novels, *The Seven Exalted Orders* and *The Grimhold Wolf*. During those discussions, I asked Carol if we might also reprint *Wee Folk and Wise*. She said yes, and so the process began again.

Unfortunately, there were several authors I had fallen out of touch with, or who had other plans for their stories. Yet, we still have an amazing and magical collection of fairy stories to share. Welcome to the second edition of *Wee Folk and Wise!* But be careful—not all of them are friendly…

Table of Contents

BEWARE THE FAIRY'S PRICE

Lillian Csernica

Alisia filled her pitcher from the clearest part of the fountain. The old beggar woman drank, then smiled. "Sweet, well-spoken child, I grant you a gift. Whenever you speak, flowers and jewels shall fall from your lips."

Indeed they did, prompting Alisia's greedy stepmother to send Kerry, her stepsister, back to the fountain. A grand noblewoman waited there, alone and in need of a drink. Kerry scorned her, too busy searching for the old beggar woman.

"Evil hearts breed evil words," the noblewoman said. "To you I give all things scaled and slimy."

And so Alisia married the Prince, and Kerry had to flee the village, the snakes and toads her only friends.

~ * ~

"Lord Uthbrey is waiting." Queen Sylvia sat on her throne, gowned in scarlet and ermine, glittering with diamonds. She arched one thin brow at Alisia. "I trust you'll be obliging?"

Alisia bowed her head, gaining a moment's freedom from all the endless smiling. Her long blonde hair had been woven into complicated braids around her tiara, giving her a headache. Her emerald satin gown was so heavy with embroidery and pearls it made her back hurt. Standing beside Alisia in his wine red doublet and trunk hose, his wavy dark hair perfect, Jeremy still looked the ideal heroic prince.

Lord Uthbrey, stout and gray and debonair, stood at the far end of the throne room with his attendants. Queen Sylvia rewarded Lord Uthbrey's attentive look with an encouraging smile. At his word, two of the pages in Lord Uthbrey's retinue brought forward a small, round table. On it sat a tall object covered with a silken veil. Lord Uthbrey approached the throne and bowed.

"His Most Royal Majesty, Wallace the Fourth, presents his compliments on the occasion of Their Highnesses' third wedding anniversary."

Lord Uthbrey lifted the silk away, revealing a slender alabaster statue. The hair and gown were bright with gilding and tiny jewels. It was Alisia herself, captured in the very essence of the fairy's curse.

"Speak, Alisia." Queen Sylvia smiled, her eyes cold. "Is it not a marvelous likeness?"

A wave of dizziness swept over Alisia. She should have been a mother by now, a normal woman with normal healthy babies. She glanced at Jeremy, that lying coward. He married Alisia at the Queen's command. On their wedding night he'd had her bound and gagged, taking her virginity with all the care he might show some drunken prostitute. In his eyes she was a freak, a pretty monster who spat out gems and flowers on demand. Monsters. A sudden wild impulse gripped Alisia, making it easier to force her lips upward in a sweet smile.

"His Majesty is most kind."

As the words passed her lips, three sapphires, a white rose, and an orchid fell. No amount of good manners and diplomatic training could prevent the gasps and astonished looks from the members of Lord Uthbrey's retinue.

"Indeed, my lord, I am overcome. You must be my companion at dinner." Alisia turned and made a deep curtsy at the throne to hide the defiance burning in her heart. "If Her Royal Majesty will allow me the pleasure."

"By all means."

Ignoring the smug satisfaction in the queen's voice, Alisia took Lord Uthbrey's offered arm, her empty heart brimming with fresh purpose.

~ * ~

While darkness still covered the land, Alisia dressed quickly, then pulled a morning robe on over her traveling gown. Tucking her feet into fleece slippers, she arranged herself in her cushioned chair and tried to look calm. The sun had just begun to lighten the eastern sky when the door opened to admit Alisia's maid Mina and a younger girl of perhaps twelve. Both girls bobbed curtsies.

"This is Lora, Your Highness."

"Good morning, Lora. Do you remember me from the village?"

Lora's brown eyes widened as she watched the flowers and gems tumble into Alisia's lap. "Yes'm. You'd pick the apples up high where us little ones couldn't reach."

"Do you remember my sister Kerry?"

Lora turned white and shied back against Mina's skirt.

"Oh, Your Highness, please!" Mina cried. "Don't go asking about her!"

"Do you know where Kerry lives?"

Lora shook her head hard.

"Your Highness, *please* —" Mina began.

"I only want to help Kerry. No one will ever know Lora told me where she is."

Mina whispered to Lora, who kept shaking her head. Alisia sorted out the clutter in her lap, letting the flowers fall into the basket beside her chair. At last Lora answered Mina's coaxing with an indistinct mumble broken by sobs and sniffles.

"She's out in the swamp, Your Highness," Mina said. "A day's ride south from the village."

Alisia shut her eyes against the unspeakable possibilities. "Thank you, Lora." She scooped up a handful of gems. "You may have one, if you like."

Lora crept forward, eyes wide. She chose a smooth round bead of milky jade. Both girls curtsied, then Mina hurried Lora out.

Alisia kicked off her slippers and laid aside her robe, then stamped into her riding boots. Her bag was packed and ready. She swung her heavy cloak around her shoulders and fastened the brooch. With luck, any servants who glimpsed her would think she was just another Malrovian guest out for an early ride. Ahead of her, the door opened.

"Aren't we busy this morning?" Queen Sylvia stood in the doorway, barring any escape. She was no less imposing in her fur-lined satin robe. Even at this hour, diamonds sparkled from her wrists and throat. "I'm told you had a visitor."

"Just a girl from my village, Your Majesty. I was feeling homesick."

Queen Sylvia regarded her with a flat, hard stare. "I can hear the truth from you, or I can get it out of the child herself."

Alisia's heart sank. "I want to find my stepsister. To help her."

"You are now a member of the Royal Family. You should be devoting your whole attention to the negotiations with Lord Uthbrey."

Alisia kept her eyes down.

"Speaking of that," Queen Sylvia went on, "after tonight's feast, you will sing, wandering from table to table, scattering your jewels and flowers among our guests. It should make for quite a charming spectacle."

Alisia kept perfectly still, denying Queen Sylvia any hint of the anger and desperation churning within her.

"You have failed utterly in your primary duty as Consort," the queen snapped, warming to her usual theme. "In three years' time you haven't shown so much as a single sign of bearing sons!"

Alisia's cheeks burned, part shame, part anger. The emptiness inside her had become a constant ache. Still, it was better this way. Far better that Alisia bore no children who would become more pawns in Queen Sylvia's endless schemes for land, wealth, and power.

"If not for this gift of yours," the queen said, "I'd have insisted Jeremy set you aside for a more fruitful wife. Since you cannot give him heirs, the very least you can do is be of this much use!"

Nagging, accusing, condemning. Just like Alisia's stepmother. Alisia raised her head and met the queen's glare.

"So I'm of no use?" She walked over to the balcony doors and flung them wide open. "Look at your royal gardens, Your Majesty, blooming with thousands of my flowers. Look at your soldiers, armed and armored thanks to the jewels I provide."

"You speak well enough when it suits you. Ungrateful words, at that."

"I never asked to be brought here! I never asked to be Your Majesty's trained monkey, spitting out trinkets for everyone you want to impress!"

"Silence!" The queen took a deep breath, smoothed one hand over her hair. "From now on, you will not leave these rooms unless and until I send for you."

With that, the queen stormed out.

Moments later Mina peeked around the edge of the doorway. "Shall I fetch your breakfast, Your Highness?"

Alisia stared after the queen, filled with a sudden stone cold hatred. Queen Sylvia could have allowed Alisia to use at least a portion of her gems to improve the lives of the common people. Better medicine, education, investments in their businesses... There was so much good Alisia could have been doing. Three years in this pretty prison had taught her one sure lesson. The queen's ultimatums yielded to her greed and vanity.

"You can fetch me Lord Uthbrey. Tell him I'd be delighted to go riding with him this very morning, but I'm afraid he'll have to ask Her Royal Majesty first."

~ * ~

Alisia tied her horse's reins to a low-hanging branch. Here the honest trees gave way to twisted oaks and blighted willows. An unhealthy stink tainted the air, the smell of swamp gas and rot. She leaned against the saddle, stiff and sore and longing for sleep. No one had expected her to run off, so it had been easy enough to escape Lord Uthbrey's riding party once they were deep in the forest. Two days' hard riding had brought her to this foul place.

Alisia peered through the tangled branches and murky light. A hovel sat wedged between two willows, its warped roof sagging under the weight of moss and fallen leaves. Smoke leaked from the crooked chimney. Fear and fatigue made Alisia doubt the wisdom of what she was about to do. She could still go back. The queen would be furious, but that would be far outweighed by her relief over the safe return of her personal treasure chest. Alisia's fists clenched. She marched up to the hovel's door and knocked on the splintered wood.

"Kerry? It's me, Alisia."

A large crack split open the upper left corner of the door. Alisia reached up to stuff two garnets, a pearl, and a tulip through it. They hit the floor with a muffled clatter. Inside the hovel a chair scraped back. The door creaked inward an inch, revealing a bloodshot blue eye.

"It is you!"

Kerry threw the door wide open. The sudden gust of fetid air made Alisia's empty stomach lurch. The three years hung on Kerry like thirty. Her face was lined and haggard, her black hair filthy. She wore stained and greasy rags. Her feet were bare, callused and muddied. Toads and snakes scrambled around her ankles in a mad rush for freedom. Alisia clapped one hand over her mouth, fighting down the urge to scream and run.

Kerry stared at her, mouth twisting with suspicion. "Why are you here? Don't tell me they threw you out, not when you can still do that." She prodded the gems and flowers with a dirty toe. Her eyebrows shot up. Her mouth fell open. "Don't tell me you're here to make it all better! After all this time, you're finally feeling guilty?"

Kerry grabbed Alisia's arm in a bruising grip and dragged her inside the hovel. The walls were covered with snakeskins. Beneath Alisia's feet crunched long, slender skeletons. One area of the floor was swept clear, down to the hard-packed dirt. Cut into the dirt was a circle bordered with snake skulls, their fangs pointing inward. Inside the circle lay patterns soaked into the dirt with—blood. It had to be blood, taken from little animals who were now nothing more than a pile of rank pelts flung into one corner. Alisia yanked her arm free and spun around. Kerry's forearm blocked the doorway. Her sudden smile frightened Alisia even more.

"You want to help me, little sister? Good. You aren't leaving here until you do."

"What do you mean?"

"I'm going to work another Summoning, only this time you'll be the one calling that fairy bitch. After all, she likes *you*."

Alisia flung herself under Kerry's arm, tumbling across the mud. She leaped up and ran, making straight for her horse. Behind her Kerry screamed a string of nonsense. Alisia's knees collapsed beneath her, sending her sprawling face down in the mud. Kerry's heavy steps squished toward her.

"Little Miss Princess, with her flowers and diamonds and pearls!" Kerry grabbed Alisia by the hair and jerked her head up. "Why do you give a damn if I live or die?"

Snakes slithered through the mud inches from Alisia's face. More small but heavy bodies crawled across her back.

"Answer me!" Kerry caught a fat black snake behind its head, thrusting it at Alisia so its fangs stuck out. Alisia's eyelids slammed shut. She shrieked until her throat was raw.

"Answer me or I'll make you eat it!"

"I just want a normal life!" Tears gushed down Alisia's cheeks. "I want someone to love *me*, not these!" She slapped at the muddy gems. "Don't you want that, Kerry? Don't you want a husband and babies and a decent, normal life?"

Kerry stared into her eyes for an endless moment. She flung away the black snake, then hauled Alisia to her feet. "I'll tell you what I want, little sister. I want everything you have. I want the palace, the prince, the pretty clothes and good food. I want it all."

"You can have it."

"Not like this, I can't." Kerry grabbed Alisia by the shoulders and shook her. "It should have been me! I was supposed to marry a prince! Mama said so! Instead she had to marry that penny-pinching mumblecrust who fathered you!"

Lizards and snakes spilled down between them. Forked tongues prodded Alisia. Cold claws scraped at her skin. She screamed, trying to twist out of Kerry's brutal grip.

"Say yes, Alisia. Say you'll do it!"

"No!"

Kerry hissed and spat. Alisia's scream died, crushed out of her by the coils of some enormous unseen snake.

"You know the fairy will come to you, Alisia. Say yes!"

"Won't be—a *witch*!"

The phantom snake squeezed inward. Alisia feared her bones would break.

"I can let it eat you, Alisia. It will swallow you slowly, bit by bit. Plenty of time for you to go mad while it drowns you in bile."

"Stop it!"

The coils crushed inward. Something covered Alisia's head like a damp, mucky hood.

"Last chance, little sister! Will you do it?"

Burning acid seared Alisia's scalp, stung her eyes, blinding her with agony. She screamed.

"*Yes!*"

The coils vanished. Alisia collapsed in the mud, sobbing.

~ * ~

Midnight found Alisia just outside the ring of snake skulls. The wavering flames of a dozen candles called evil shadows from every corner. The candles burned with a stink that brought unwelcome thoughts about the exact source of their tallow. Inside the ring sat two rough wooden dishes. One held entrails and the other blood.

Kerry stood on the far side of the circle. "Remember, no matter what you see, stay out of the circle."

Alisia nodded. A cold, rusty horseshoe hung round her neck on a strip of tattered cloth. The iron should protect her. If not, its weight made it a useful weapon.

Kerry chanted in a low, husky voice. The candle flames streamed upward, then settled back again. A wet, rotten stench rose up from the floor. Two small creatures popped up inside the circle.

The first was pink and hairless as a baby mouse, its one yellow eye glaring out of its forehead. It plunged its snout into the bowl of blood. The other had greasy black fur split by a gaping mouth full of jagged teeth. It fell on the entrails, chomping and slurping. Alisia shrieked. Kerry knelt and cooed at the little horrors. They chittered and huffed at her. She looked up at Alisia.

"Tell them. Now."

"I—I want to talk to the fairy who put the spells on us. Bring her here, right now. Tell her Princess Alisia needs her."

The two creatures whuffled at each other, then disappeared.

"Will they do it?" Alisia asked.

"They'd better. Or it will be them in the bowls next time."

Moment after moment passed. Kerry crouched at the edge of the circle, staring into the center with eyes full of mad, desperate hope. A burst of rainbow brilliance made Alisia cry out and clap her hands to her eyes.

"I warned you, you wretched little hag!" That voice. Cool, haughty, infinitely superior. "I told you never to lure me here with that name again!"

Alisia lowered her hands. The fairy stood there, her silky white hair bound into a coronet braid, wearing pale lavender gown embroidered with wildflowers and a silver circlet set with the milky gleam of moonstones. At her feet lay what was left of the two little monsters.

The fairy stared at Alisia. "You? Here?" Her amethyst eyes narrowed and her lip curled in disgust. "So, the hateful sister and the virtuous sister are reunited? How things do change."

"Please," Alisia said. "Take back your gifts."

"Why should I? You earned them." The fairy glared at Kerry. "You most of all!"

Kerry's hatred simmered in her eyes. Her mouth opened.

"Silence!" The fairy snatched up the hairy monster and jammed it into Kerry's mouth.

Kerry fell over backward, gagging. The fairy stepped out of the circle and stood glaring down at her. Kerry looked from the fairy to the circle and back, eyes widening. The fairy smiled, thin and cold.

"Did you really think your petty little blood magic would bind one of us? I am the Countess Benaille. I should kill you for your presumption."

"Leave her alone!" Alisia cried. "What she is, you made her! Just break the spells and we'll never call on you again."

"Why should I? You both lead the lives you deserve. You in a palace, her in a sty."

"I do not deserve the life you've given me! You've made me a trained monkey, a freak, a glorified court jester!"

Countess Benaille frowned. "Once I sought to reward virtue and punish vanity. I see before me a wasted effort. That one is no better than she ever was. But you." She bent to pick up a single white rose lying on the dirt. Breathing in its scent, she shook her head. "So ungrateful you dare insult me. Spoiled, selfish, haughty. Everything I once knew you were not."

Alisia met that amethyst stare with every ounce of strength she'd built up facing Queen Sylvia. "You said you wanted to reward virtue and punish vanity. Is that true? Or are you just one more lord's daughter who likes to torture helpless animals?"

Countess Benaille flung the rosebud into flowers piled at Alisia's feet. The flowers withered, shrank, crumbled to dust. "Prove me wrong, Princess. Prove virtue still dwells in your heart. Give your gift to your 'sister,' and take hers in exchange."

Alisia gasped. Those horrible scaly monsters crawling out of her own mouth? She made herself think of Kerry before her courage failed her completely. Kerry would take her place in the palace. Kerry would have all the lovely things she'd ever dreamed of. Kerry would very likely sass Queen Sylvia into some kind of fit. Alisia would make a new home for herself, with hard work and patience. She was no stranger to either.

"I will." She watched the rose and tourmaline fall. "Tell me what to do."

"A simple matter. Like so many enchantments, it must be sealed with a kiss."

Alisia hardened her heart against the terror of it. She walked around the circle to where Kerry still lay. Kerry looked up at her. Again Kerry's eyes held that wild, frantic hope. Alisia knelt beside her and smoothed Kerry's filthy hair back from her brow.

"Tell Father I love him. He'd best forget about me."

~ * ~

Alisia stood in the throne room a few steps behind Kerry. A

long afternoon spent scrubbing away the layers of grime had taken years off Kerry. She wore a new dress of dark brown wool. Her braided hair now gleamed with red highlights.

Queen Sylvia sat on her throne, frowning in deep distrust. Jeremy lounged beside her on a cushioned chair, fondling the ears of his favorite hunting dog.

"You claim the fairy took Alisia away to the place where she'd already hidden you," the queen said, "then told you it was time the gifts were traded."

"That's right, Your Majesty." Kerry nodded. "She said something about magic and the laws of balance."

Queen Sylvia watched the rain of gems and flowers patter down around Kerry's feet. "Since when do fairies care about rules and laws and such?"

"I wouldn't know, Your Majesty. All I know is, here I am." Kerry caught a few gems in her fist and rattled them like dice, making the assembled courtiers wince.

Queen Sylvia stared at Alisia with an intensity meant to strip her bare. "Have you nothing to add?"

Alisia shook her head.

"You do realize what this would mean? Your marriage annulled, your rooms given over to your stepsister, your life as Royal Consort at an end?"

Alisia nodded.

"Will you not say a single word? You put on quite a display the last time you stood before me."

Kerry took a step forward. "You really don't want her to speak, Your Majesty. Not unless you want to watch what happens when a hooded swamp rattler bites someone."

All the courtiers backed away. Some already glanced down in distaste, wearing that look Alisia had seen all too often on Jeremy's face. As if reading her thoughts, Queen Sylvia turned to Jeremy.

"Jeremy? Have you anything to say? After all, Alisia is your wife."

Jeremy gave both Alisia and Kerry the briefest glance, then shrugged. "Hardly makes much of a difference."

"So he's like that, is he?" Kerry muttered under her breath.

Alisia smiled. If revenge had been her main purpose, she couldn't have done better than wishing Kerry on Jeremy and the queen.

Queen Sylvia clapped her hands. Two of the guards stepped forward. She fixed Alisia with a brilliant smile. "Throw the ungrateful little wretch in the dungeon."

"What?" Kerry cried. "Why? You have me! You don't need her anymore!"

"My dear ignorant peasant girl, she has lived under this roof for three years as the wife of Prince Jeremy, who will one day be king. No other man will ever touch her."

Kerry scowled. She thrust both hands at the guards and snarled. The guards dropped to their knees, clutching their heads.

"Stop it!"

Alisia's voice rang out. Her hands flew to her mouth. A muddy lizard and a bright red snake struck the flagstones at her feet. They struggled together, fighting free to slither back between Alisia's ankles. She screamed, bringing forth even more scaly monsters. The room whirled around her. Triumphant laughter rang in her ears. Queen Sylvia or Countess Benaille? It hardly made much of a difference.

~ * ~

Alisia woke to find herself lying on a wooden bench inside a cold, damp closet made of stone. Ruddy light came from the one torch that burned in the corridor, showing her the bars across the little window in the door. She sat up, tried to stand. The stiffness in her joints told her hours must have passed. She wondered how long she'd have to wait. It was only a matter of time before the queen had her executed.

Outside, footsteps and voices came toward the cell. The ring of keys jingled in the lock. The door swung open, revealing Queen Sylvia.

"I want a private word with her. Private, you understand?"

"But—Your Majesty, the snakes—"

"Our dear little princess wouldn't hurt me."

The guard hurried away. The queen stared after him for a moment, then turned a cold look on Alisia.

"At a loss for words, my dear?"

The queen's features blurred. Her midnight blue gown rippled away into lavender trimmed with glittering dewdrops. Countess Benaille now stood in the doorway. Despite her shock, Alisia said nothing.

"Did you really believe the queen would just let you go back to your village, carding wool and whelping some farmer's brats?" Countess Benaille shook her head. "You're a fool. But you are an honorable one. I'll give you that."

Alisia turned her face away. Flattery from a fairy was even more dangerous than scorn. Countess Benaille stepped inside the cell.

"I could get you out of here, you know. If we came to a satisfactory arrangement."

Alisia sighed, sinking down on the wooden bench. She was so tired of living according to everyone else's whims. All she wanted was to go home, wherever that might be.

"Come back to my court with me," Countess Benaille said. "Attend me as my lady-in-waiting. Perhaps you'll catch the eye of a fairy lord." Countess Benaille sat down beside Alisia and laid an arm around her shoulders. "Your babies are waiting for you."

Alisia's head jerked up.

"It's neither my fault nor yours," Countess Benaille said. "The truth is dear Jeremy spends more than just his time away from you. Spends so much he's no use to any woman hoping for a child."

So it *wasn't* Alisia's fault! Relief gave way to rage. Alisia sprang up and lunged out through the open doorway. Invisible hands closed on her arms and spun her around, pinning her against the wall opposite the cell. The cell door slammed shut. The big iron key turned in the lock. Countess Benaille screeched, pounding her fists against the door. She screamed again, this time in pain, and shrank back, whimpering.

Kerry popped into sight right beside Alisia, holding a black cord strung with snake bones, feathers, and what looked like tiny eyes. She stepped up to the cell door and laughed.

"You forgot about the iron, didn't you? It blinded you just long enough."

"You will suffer for this." Countess Benaille's voice was icy. "I promise you that."

"Maybe, but you'll get yours first." Kerry held out the necklace to Alisia. "Put this on. Wear it as far as the borders of the kingdom, then burn it."

Alisia pointed upstairs, then spread her hands in a wondering gesture. Kerry grinned.

"I'll tell the old bat I thought the fairy might come to rescue you. You'd already escaped, but I got here in time to trap the fairy in the cell."

Kerry dug into the bag hanging off her shoulder and pulled out a large pouch, then pushed it into Alisia's hands. Alisia recognized the feel of it, heavy with gems. Eyes brimming with happy tears, Alisia clasped Kerry to her and kissed her cheek. Kerry blushed.

"Now get going!"

"Alisia!" Countess Benaille snapped. "Free me! Leave me here and there will be no escape from those who will avenge me!"

"Go on!" Kerry said. "I'll take care of her." She grinned. "Iron shackles. Iron knives and pincers and mulling rods. I can't wait."

"*Alisia!*" Raw panic colored Countess Benaille's voice. "I gave you three years of royalty! Now I've given it to your stepsister as well! Let me *out!*"

Alisia hesitated. She clenched her eyes shut and braced herself. "Break the spell on me." Scaly rustlings slid down her skirt. She swallowed, tried to breathe normally. "And swear all of you will leave Kerry alone. Then I'll let you out."

"No!" Kerry cried. "She's mine! You can't let her go!"

"Let me out!"

Alisia stepped up to the cell door. In Countess Benaille's eyes she saw the same look Kerry had worn, that same mad, desperate hope for freedom and peace. Satisfied, Alisia gripped the iron key.

"Swear first," Alisia said. "Then break the spell."

"Very well." Countess Benaille scowled and spoke in a mocking singsong. "From this moment on I swear on my life to abandon Kerry to her own stupidity and see to it my people meddle with her no further."

"And?"

"Let me out. The iron interferes."

Alisia opened the door. Back stiff, eyes narrowed to slits, Countess Benaille walked out of the cell one dignified step at a time. She covered Alisia's mouth with one hand, then snapped her fingers.

"There."

"Thank you." To Alisia's intense relief, nothing but breath left her lips.

"Your troubles are far from over," Countess Benaille hissed. "This is all the help you'll have from me." She vanished in another flash of rainbow light.

Just then the guard rounded the corner. "Here now, what's all this noise? Where's Her Majesty?"

Kerry pushed Alisia behind her. "Just let her go."

"Her Majesty will have my head!"

"Tell *me* what you need," Kerry said. "You'll have it, I promise you."

The guard watched the gems and flowers fall. Once more Alisia saw desperate hope in the eyes of another person.

"It's my little girl." The guard spoke in a rush, glancing back over his shoulder. "Her leg's not right. Can't walk, can't run and play —"

Kerry nodded. "The Royal Physician will see her tomorrow. Now keep anyone else away."

The guard made a hasty bow and darted back the way he'd come.

"Remember." Kerry held out the revolting necklace to Alisia. "Wear this as far as the borders of the kingdom, then burn it."

Alisia nodded. She was oddly reluctant to leave Kerry. The ordeal had brought them close, far closer than they had ever been. "With Father away, you're all the family I have."

"You're wasting time."

Alisia's heart sank. "I—I suppose I was foolish to hope you might feel any closeness to me. You have what you've always wanted. A sister was never part of that."

Alisia turned away, working up the nerve to slip the horrid necklace down around her neck. It was time to begin the long walk toward her new life.

"Alisia."

Alisia glanced back. Kerry held out a blue glass marble half the size of a hen's egg.

"Take this. It will help you find your father."

Alisia took the marble, staring in open-mouthed wonder. "But —but why? I thought you hated both of us."

Kerry looked away, her eyes wet with welling tears. "You came back for me. You wanted the fairy to break the spell on me as well." Kerry forced herself to look Alisia in the eye. "You didn't have to do that."

Alisia clasped her sister in a fervent hug.

~ * ~ * ~

Ms. Csernica's fiction has appeared in *Weird Tales*, *Fantastic Stories*, and *Jewels of Darkover*. Born in San Diego, Ms. Csernica is a genuine California native. She currently resides in the Santa Cruz mountains with her husband, two sons, and three cats.

Visit her at lillian888.wordpress.com.

children in the sky

Michael Lee Johnson

There is a full moon,
Distant in this sky tonight,

Gray planets planted
On an aging, white face.

Children, living and dead,
Love the moon with tiny hearts.

Those already in heaven take a gold thread,
drop the moon down for us all to see.

Those alive with us look out their
bedroom windows tonight.

We smile, then pray, then sleep.

~ * ~ * ~

Michael Lee Johnson, USA & Canadian citizen, now Chicagoland area, is an internationally published poet in 45 countries, a song lyricist, has several published poetry books, has been nominated for 7 Pushcart Prize awards, and 6 Best of the Net nominations.

He has over 297 YouTube poetry videos as of 11-2023. www.youtube.com/user/poetrymanusa/videos

OFFERING

Kara Race-Moore

I could still hear the wheels from Boston's uniquely inefficient subway system squeaking above my head as I was ushered into the Gathering Hall. The area was crowded with creatures of all kinds, all looking toward me. The king and queen were easy to spot on their thrones at the far end of the room. Not a flicker of emotion showed on their perfect faces.

My guide smiled up at me. When he had appeared in my room earlier this evening, he had introduced himself as Bramblecock, a kobold—a goblin of good Germanic family on his mother's side, he had explained, who had immigrated to the States back when Bismarck began modernizing Prussia.

"Welcome to the Unseelie court," he said to me now.

"What is this?" asked a woman at the front of the crowd. At a glance, she appeared to be a prim matron dressed in late Elizabethan, almost Puritan fashion. Every inch of skin below her chin was layered, ruffled and laced in gray, white and black. A neat chignon of twisting green garter snakes above her pale face jarred the appearance of humanity. Cold water rushed beneath my skin. I would have to tell my therapist that fear made a better cure for depression than Lexapro.

"My dear Mistress of the Revels, I have brought the Offering," my guide said to the woman. "As you ordered, Joanya."

The sly note in his voice suggested an inside joke, one I was as far outside as anything from the popular crowd at school.

"Come, come, Master Bramblecock," Joanya said. "This one will not do at all. A creature from the light? You mock us with this Offering."

At my side, Bramblecock grinned with a mouth full of far too many teeth. He grabbed my left wrist with long blue fingers and yanked up the sleeve of the long-sleeved top I wore despite summer's heat. He shoved my forearm into full view, showing the angry straight red lines.

"*This* one has felt pain," he leered.

The entire court laughed, as if this was the hilarious punch line to a dirty joke. I was so frozen with shock, I wasn't sure I was still breathing.

"I'm sure King Serkan and Queen Ilmacay will appreciate this choice," Bramblecock said.

"Oh, but look—it is uneven," said a skinny reptilian creature with punk-like pink spikes on its domed head, which sounded neither male nor female. It had sidled up to my other side and pulled back the other sleeve to show a smooth expanse of skin.

"I can fix that," said another, a female who looked almost, but indefinably not, human. Her outfit was half Renaissance armor and half the height of current French fashion. Elaborately embroidered gauntlets gave her tiger-like claws. The woman came close enough to delicately run a clawed finger over each scar on the left arm.

"Five," she murmured. Then, quick as thought, she slashed my right arm and left a row of five bleeding lines.

I screamed. The cuts burned as if my whole arm had been dunked in a vat of acid. It was nothing like the feeling of release that had come from cutting myself with the shard of broken glass I kept in my jewel box. I thrashed, but couldn't get out of their grasp.

"Let me go!" I wailed.

The courtiers laughed at my fierce struggle to get free of the grasping, clutching hands. Up on the dais, the queen allowed a smirk to break the illusion of a face carved from marble. She glanced at her husband, asking something with a single arched eyebrow. He responded with a barely perceptible shrug.

There were two knights flanking the king and queen, a woman in black armor next to the king and a man in white armor next to the queen. The man's shield had an eagle in flight on it, beak open in a wordless scream of attack.

"Sir Aleron," said the queen lazily, "go fetch this creature and bring it to us."

"Your slightest wish is my most urgent command, my dark lady," he said with a bow, then marched down the dais and through the crowd. He grabbed my arm and escorted me to the dais.

"Bow to the king and queen of the Unseelie Court," the knight growled, enforcing the request with a hard shove to my back. He almost sent me sprawling and forced me to lean forward in a semblance of respect.

Queen Ilmacay looked me over. She had a pair of wings like a Monarch butterfly, which opened and shut slowly as she considered me.

"She will do," she declared grandly, as if bestowing largesse.

"Say thank you," snapped the knight.

I stood silent, frozen again. I felt something on my hand and looked down. A few drops of blood trickled down my arm from the clawing, but at least the pain had faded.

"Go on." He prodded me painfully in the ribs with a thick, gauntleted finger.

"No," I snapped, glancing around wildly to glare at the queen, the knight, and my errant tour guide. "You didn't say I'd be humiliated," I accused Bramblecock. From what he had said, I thought I would receive respect and reward for joining as the court's resident Human Artist, as he had phrased the title of the position he offered. I hadn't expected this circus show, where I was the main attraction.

Joanya laughed. "Oh, what did my little errand-runner promise this one?"

He grinned his many-toothed grim. "Many things," he said slyly.

"But...but...but..." I sputtered. "But you can't lie!" I finally managed to get out, feeling betrayed by all the books I had grown up with.

The whole court laughed again.

"It is true that lying is the province of *humans*." Joanya pronounced my species name like it was something filthy. "But the truth viewed up close and seen from far away are two very different creatures. The stories you read may have told you we cannot lie, but did they not also tell you we feel free to present the truth however we see fit?" She sounded very amused.

"Crap," was all I managed to say. I thought back to the original conversation with Bramblecock.

"But aren't the Unseelie the bad guys?" I had asked when he explained who and what he was and where he had come from. "Evil fairies, the ones that cause trouble?"

He had made a derisive motion with his hand, flicking away the allegation.

"Don't think of it as good and bad, think of it more as day and night. Most of what you've heard is Seelie propaganda from the human poets and minstrels they've hosted. But we need humans at our revels, too. We lack the spark that only a human artist has. Come see our side of the story," he had

cajoled. "You wish to be a writer. Come see something to write about."

He had gone on with honeyed words about what a rare thing it was for a human to be invited to a fairy court and how wonderful in particular tonight's revels would be. With nothing else to do that night but stare at the blank page of paper that was my life, I went with him, down into the bottom of the city and depths I never knew it had. Rapidly reviewing what he had said, I realized he hadn't said anything specific about the experience being good for me.

Now the kobold laughed and said to Joanya, "This is why I love to court the clever ones. They always manage to cut themselves with their own tongues!"

"Enough." The king spoke for the first time. "We must prepare for the ceremony."

Suddenly I found myself quite on my own as everyone ignored me and went about their business. Free to walk around and treated as though I was invisible. It was the school cafeteria all over again.

There was a buffet table in one corner. I walked up to the table, wondering if anyone was going to stop me. Except for the disturbingly similar trio of girls with hair like seaweed and puddles of water around their feet, who gave me a smug once-over, I was still being ignored.

The table was heaped with the expected mountains of shining fruits, baskets of bread, platters loaded with juicy meat cuts that didn't look fully cooked, pitchers of dark red and golden amber liquids. Other exotic-looking dishes I couldn't decipher included little pots of colored powders. Leaves and flowers were scattered in some sort of gothic Martha Stewart arrangement. I hovered uncertainly, wondering if the stories about eating fairy food were true.

"Go on, have a bite of something, dearie," said a voice near my knees. I looked down at what could have been a tiny, wizened old woman except for the fact that she looked slightly furry. And dusty. Like an old cleaning lady crossed with a dust ball. She stretched out a disturbingly long arm that somehow reached the table above her, and snatched up one of the fruits.

"Apple?" she asked, holding the bright red fruit out to me.

A thousand alarm bells rang in my head. "No, thank you," I squeaked, and quickly moved back into the crowd. I was jostled by a woman wearing a blindfold whose bottom half was a serpent's tail. Then I bumped into the glassy-eyed woman with green and blond hair and skin so heavily tattooed that I wasn't sure of her original skin color. She was wearing streetwalker-from-Hell attire and earrings of heavy gold ingots.

I wandered toward one of the walls just for the simple feeling of something solid to lean against. I ended up sliding down into a sitting position, amazed to have fallen down the rabbit hole and be just as bored as back at school.

Something near my foot caught my eye. It was so out of place that I stared at it for several long moments, my mind unable to register what I was looking at. I picked it up. It was a used and discarded Starbucks coffee cup. The green and white logo couldn't be anything else. The top was missing, and there was a dry crusty brown ring at the bottom.

"Her Majesty's grande triple-shot hazelnut syrup organic milk dry Americano," rattled off someone to my right. "You would not believe the trouble a courtier will go through to bring her this whenever she demands her fix."

The voice sounded highly amused. It belonged to a young man kneeling next to me, with goat horns poking through his curly dark hair and vaguely horse-like ears. He didn't look as high-class as the rest. More like someone from a different group, just there for the party. He wore an intricately embroidered vest worthy of a 19th century gypsy, over a hairy bare chest and ordinary-looking jeans. I couldn't tell what kind of feet he had.

"The fey drink coffee?" I asked, incredulous.

"What do you think we sup upon—virgins and starlight?"

I glanced at the buffet table and shrugged. "I don't know. Before tonight, I would have guessed ambrosia and that flatbread J. R. R. Tolkein made such a big deal about."

He laughed in my face. "Him. He was in love with his own voice. But we fey all have notorious sweet-teeth. Any kind of sugar will make us quite happy, and we will cheerfully consume any dairy we can get our hands on. Which is hard, as bovines hate us—hence the fact that we have historically blessed any farmer thoughtful enough to leave us a dish of milk on the doorstep. And, we are all nuts about caffeine. When you humans managed to combine all three in your quaint little coffee chains... Well, you can imagine." Nodding toward the entrance, he added, "Just look at the gift a latecomer has brought."

I looked in the direction of the entrance. A man with slick, ruby-red hair and marble-white skin, wearing a brightly patterned loincloth, had just arrived and was attracting a horde of the guests. The crowd parted for a moment, and I could see he had a large box in each hand. Both bore the unmistakable logo of Dunkin Donuts. One of the boxes was the flat rectangle used for a dozen doughnuts. The other was a fat, square 'Box-O-Joe,' the grown-up version of a juice box that, siren-like, promised a dozen cups worth of piping hot coffee.

"Who's he?" I asked, amazed that for all their magic a simple doughnut appeared to be highly prized.

"That's Bellguzzle, a cousin of the king who's only just back in favor with their majesties after some incident involving a mortal girl. I don't know what, exactly; rumors vary. A very wise young sidhe he is, too, to have brought such a treat tonight. Those will be gone faster than a pixie can steal eggs." He looked longingly at the bearer of sweets and caffeine, but made no move to get up. Maybe Bellguzzle was in a cooler clique than him.

A sidhe noblewoman, with skin as white as Bellguzzle's but wearing infinitely more clothing in the form of a Marie Antoinette-style dress done in forest colors, poured coffee from the box into a pair of silver goblets and brought them to the dais, where the king and queen drank with reverence.

Meanwhile, the goatman went on, "If Starbucks knew we existed, they could take over the Fey Realms far more easily and faster than they have spread over the Human Realm."

"That's saying a lot," I said, thinking of how many Starbuckses there were in Boston alone. The group of courtiers now all had doughnuts in their hands. "So, are you part of the Unseelie court?"

"Nope," he said cheerfully. "Just a solitary fey crashing the party. A lot of solitary fey come to Unseelie rituals."

I nodded, then tilted my head back until my forehead nearly touched the wall. "Jesus Christ, this is insane."

"Master Gylmyne," said someone above us, "I believe our... guest is wanted by their majesties."

I looked up. Joanya stood over us, looking annoyed about something. Past her, I could see the milling around had turned into some semblance of order. People seemed to be forming lines. I got up and was directed to the front, right behind their majesties.

We walked through twisting tunnels, some lit with torches and held up by wooden timbers. Others had electric lights and metal beams that looked like they had been 'borrowed' from the Boston Public Works Department.

At first I wondered if ogres or trolls or some other sort of monster would jump out from one or another of the many turns we went through, until I realized I was traveling with the monsters. This made me both more and less afraid.

A pair of fairies no bigger than dragonflies flitted above my head as we walked. One landed on my shoulder and began to whisper in a deceptively childlike voice.

"How do you know this is not a dream? How do you *know?* How do you know you don't hold an empty bottle of spirits or an empty jar of pills or a blood-red blade in your dreaming hand right now? Is this all some realistic nightmare before your pathetic little human brain shuts down?"

I stumbled, my arms refusing to respond to my screaming mental command to brush this psychotic moth away.

"Why now, even *now*, your last remaining drops of life could be spilling from your body, pooling into a crimson lake for some innocent to find." I could hear the grin in its voice as it continued. "I'm sure there will be a touching little funeral, though I doubt anyone will be able to find time in their busy schedules to come."

"Enough," said Joanya from behind me. She flicked the fairy away.

After what felt like miles of underground warrens, we came to a large open space. Roots of plants among timbered beams made the vaulted ceiling. The floor was not of packed dirt, like the tunnels, but marbled square tiles of black and white, like a giant chessboard. I wondered if we were still underneath Boston.

At the far end was another set of thrones. The king and queen seated themselves, and everyone else took places around the hall in what seemed to be a pre-determined manner. Joanya took a firm grip on my arm and walked me to the very center of the hall. She stepped back, and I felt every eye on me as I stood alone.

A woman who looked like a walking tree stepped forward, holding something in her barky, leafy hands. Turning her back to me, she addressed the court.

"The seventh year has come again, and so we, the Unseelie

Court of New Avalon, founded with and underneath the foundations of the City on a Hill, seek the human who will provide us with the energy we need."

She turned to look me directly in the eye.

"Human child, you have been chosen for this mighty task, to give us what we need for our power. We humbly request access to the rays of your pulsing human spirit, that wellspring of creation. Do you accept?"

I was lost in her words, entranced by the idea that they needed me to be the sun on their solar panels, as it were.

"Yes," I said without thinking. My voice echoed, and a light, purple mist enveloped the hall.

"Then offer us something tangible, as Will of your Word," she said persuasively. I could hear the capital letters in her solemn voice. She offered a silver dagger that looked sharp enough to slash through rock, and a silver dish that abruptly brought me out of my reverie. It looked like the platter at church used to hold the sacramental bread during Communion.

I thought quickly. Blood was what she meant, but the wording left the decision to me. I had a very bad feeling about the consequences if I spilled my blood. Last chance to do something smart. What on earth did I have to offer?

A sudden burst of inspiration from crime shows and fantasy stories flashed through my head. I held out my hand for the knife. Instead of slashing at the skin on my arm, as I'm sure everyone wanted, I pulled on my ponytail and sawed at the hair, cutting above the plastic tie to keep it together in one clump. I dropped the fist-full of brown hair into the dish and was surprised how short it looked, cut apart from my body.

I spoke in what I hoped was a formal, ceremonial manner. "I offer days of taking medications and I offer nights of, uh, inhaled hazy smoke and…and…" I stammered, trying to think of a suitably mystical way to describe getting drunk. "…And the *liquid fire* that burned my throat as I drank it to try and make the demons in my own head go away. All are encapsulated and recorded here in my, uh, shorn locks. The mind can forget, but the body remembers, and I give that remembering to you."

There was a moment of stunned silence. Then, "You offer us the *past*," Joanya hissed. Her snake hair writhed in turmoil.

"Yes," I gasped, my skin ice cold and my stomach churning.

"Poor fare, indeed," said the queen, "but very neatly done." Louder, she declaimed, "We accept the Offering."

There was general grumbling, then a noise like an underwater explosion. A blinding flash followed. I was knocked down by some sort of wind.

I woke to find myself staring at the familiar sight of the marbled front entrance to the Boston Public Library. I was sitting on one of the benches in Copley Square, directly across from the library. Someone was sitting next to me. I turned and was not entirely surprised to see the goatman, Gylmyne.

"Good morning," he said cheerfully.

"What time is it?" I asked, confused by the fact that it looked to be the absolute middle of the night and there were no signs of life. True, Boston is *not* the city that never sleeps. It's more of a 'city-that-gets-its-proper-eight-hours-of-sleep-thank-you-very-much.' Still, it seemed unnaturally quiet.

"It's about three a.m." He sipped an over-sized iced coffee.

"Then where'd you get that?" I wondered how I could be so distracted by a minor detail considering everything that had happened.

"There's an all-night Dunkin Donuts on Boylston Street," he said nonchalantly, and slurped happily on the straw. "It's mostly why I volunteered to bring you back to the Human Realm."

"The people at the counter didn't freak out when they saw a guy with horns stroll in with an unconscious chick?" I asked, still insanely caught up with this detail.

"One, it was two thirty in the morning. I'm sure I'm not the strangest thing they've seen working that shift. Two, whenever I wander into your realm these days, I just make sure to mention the award I got for my costume at the comic convention, and no one lifts an eyebrow. You, I told them, had drunk too much and passed out. I related how I had to fight several other cosplayers at the con for the honor of carrying the fair lady home." He seemed to relish using the geeky words.

"So… What happened with the ceremony?" I forced myself back to the more important issue of the Unseelie Court, rather than asking where he had learned about cosplay.

"For someone who had absolutely no clue what was going on, you did very well."

I touched my much-shortened hair gingerly. It was going to take some getting used to. "They wanted my blood, didn't they?"

"Yes, *we* did," he said coldly, but then smiled, cheerful as ever. "The hair will suffice. A seven-year diet will probably do us good. We've grown fat on mortal misery."

"What happens to me now?"

"Well, we've eaten your past, but the future's all yours." He slurped the bottom of his cup's contents noisily, then pitched it into the nearest trash bin. "I'm off. Good luck, human child."

And without so much as a clap of thunder or blast of smoke, he disappeared.

~ * ~ * ~

Kara Race-Moore studied history at Simmons College as an excuse to read about the soap opera lives of British royals. She worked in educational publishing, casting the molds for the minds of future generations, but has since moved into the more civilized world of litigation. She writes horror, fantasy and science fiction stories, many inspired by her study of history. She currently lives in Los Angeles, the land where fact and fiction tend to blur. She can be found at: https://kararacemoore.wordpress.com/

uNÒER The ROSES

Elizabeth Guizzetti

Autumn sun filtered through the fingerprint-covered glass and reflected off her desk, but it wasn't enough to warm Madena. Gone were the long days of summer swim lessons and playing in the sandbox with her little sister.

She glanced up at the clock. Another minute ticked by. Trembling fingers held her stylus perpendicular to her tablet and tears scorched her eyes, but she would not give her classmates or teachers the satisfaction of seeing the weirdo cry again. Free Writing Exercises was going to be her favorite subject, but Mr. Davis and Ms. Jefferson said her poems and stories were too fanciful and flighty.

No one cared about unicorns or fairies. Nor had a single one of her classmates ever found the gateway where fairies entered this dimension, or crawled into the basement to stare at the slick, sticky mass of fairy flesh that the hunter spider left behind after its meal. She shivered as she remembered how other fairies ganged up on the poor creature. It had died screaming as they tore out its eight legs.

Ma always said, "Fairies are vindictive."

When she tried to write about it, Mr. Davis warned that he would call her parents if she wrote about such violence again. Kids who wrote about their parents' divorces got all the attention, but Ma and Papi were always giggling with their secret jokes and tickles. They even kissed. It was so gross. Even Lobo Loco didn't like it.

"That's it. Lobo!"

Madena's stylus flew across the screen:

After Ma and Papi think my sister and I are in bed, they run around the backyard and tickle and kiss. Lobo Loco is always put in my room, because he doesn't like their games. He won't sleep. All he does is pace, whine, and wait by the door until Papi lets him out. He wants to sleep at Ma's feet in her bed. Even though, Ma and Papi claim Lobo Loco is the family's dog, Lobo Loco loves Ma best. He is her dog.

She paused and chewed the end of her stylus. Honestly, Lobo's whining was more annoying than anything, but Ms. Jefferson and Mr. Davis wanted feelings so she wrote, *It makes me sad.*

This was it. They had to like this essay. Mr. Davis might like her essay so much, he would even read it to the class and then say she was brave like the kids with divorced parents.

The bell rang. She slowly followed the others outside for recess. She wanted to climb the monkey bars, but girls in Second Grade Advanced Learning Opportunities stood at the wall near the bathroom where the fifth and sixth graders hung out. Fifth and sixth graders were cool. Some even wore lipstick and nail polish.

In order to get their attention, the girls spoke with words their big sisters used. Today it was *patriarchal society* and *marketed gender roles*. Madena had no idea what they were spewing out of their smug upturned lips, but she was pretty sure girls were not supposed to like pink though her classmates were bedecked in t-shirts with flutter sleeves and as many sparkly gems as one could fit on her chest. Pink was bad, but apparently purple and red were okay. Her own t-shirt was orange with a blue spotted dinosaur that Papi embroidered. She hoped that was okay.

"I like every color. My room's filled with rainbows."

Nobody responded, but a fifth grader bent down and added blue to her lips. "To match your dinosaur."

Trying to be heard over the prattle, she said, "You know what I really like? I love that all colors become white and no colors mean black, but it didn't work with crayons or paints. That just turned everything muddy and brown."

The other girls stared.

"Madi, you're so marbles-free."

The insult was followed by a cackle and a push into the concrete wall, then a half-dozen twittering laughs. The older girls sent them annoyed looks.

She gave a fake laugh, shrugged, and chose her words carefully to match their smug manner. "I know it's just light refraction."

The second push was more playful than hard. Hopefully, they thought she just made a stupid joke. Even a failed joke was better than being marbles-free.

Their laughter was interrupted by Ms. Jefferson's bark. "Madi García, come in here, please!"

The girls twittered again. Not knowing what she had done wrong, she slunk into the classroom. Ms. Jefferson pointed at Mr. Davis's desk. Madi slowly approached him.

His face was stern as he gestured at his monitor. "What's the meaning of this?"

She glanced at the first sentence. "It's my free-writing." And clenched the hem of her t-shirt to hold in her sadness. Even before he spoke, his face told her he didn't like it.

He snapped, "This is not an appropriate subject for a girl your age."

"But other kids talk about their dogs," she sniffed and wiped her nose. "I-I tried to write brave, like you said."

He glanced at Ms. Jefferson and sighed. "Sit at your desk and think about what you did. It's time to speak with your parents… And wipe off that stuff off your face." He handed her a tissue.

Nodding, Madena went to her desk and laid her head in her arms. She didn't think about it. She thought about fairies, how Ma taught her to make rainbows with the hose, and how every color makes white.

Across the room, Ms. Jefferson scolded her mother on the phone. While she couldn't hear her mother's replies, her teacher's voice seemed to grow colder. They were to have a conference.

Feeling its cool plastic top pressing against her cheek, Madena inhaled deeply, and forced herself not to cry. She was tired of crying about Second Grade Advanced Learning Opportunities.

At least, after recess, they had a nutritious snack and math workbooks. Math was easier, because there was no wrong answer. Madena liked using clock faces and pattern blocks to solve the problems. It was easy to forget about always being in trouble, and being marbles-free.

Most days, there would be a torturous bus ride home, but after the bell rang and the kids filed out, Ma came in with Beca who proudly exclaimed, "Hi Madi! Hi, Ms. Jefferson and Mr. Davis. I'm Beca. I read *Cat in the Hat* to Mama, all by myself. I'm gonna sit here and be very quiet during the meeting. Mama said we'll have ice cream if I'm good. Wanna color?"

She plopped down at the desk beside Madena with her box of crayons and smudged spiral bound notebook. Ignoring the adults, Beca began scribbling rainbows on her paper.

"Four was a good age," Madena said, and focused on her reading assignment, *Nim's Island*. She wanted to relax into another girl's adventures all alone on the deserted island. However, class had been warned not to read ahead, they must only read pages 36 to 52. It took her all of ten minutes. She glanced over at the adults. Ma was still talking to her teachers.

"Perhaps Madi would be better served in a remedial class," Mr. Davis said. "She's highly creative and intelligent, but behind socially."

"Is there any class work she struggles with?" Ma asked.

Furious tears burned her eyes, but Madena focused on her vocabulary list from the book. She couldn't believe her classmates didn't understand words like 'chasm' or 'whorly.' Did teachers ever listen to kids, or was this just another stupid thing they made up?

She wanted to warn her little sister to not become five. At five, Beca would be shipped off to kindergarten. Just stop. Because after five comes six and after six is seven. Seven was too old to believe in fairies, even though Madena knew they existed.

Tooth fairies collected teeth. Little elves helped cobblers fix shoes and built toys for Santa. Flower fairies in Ma's garden helped bees pollinate. There were too many stories for them all to be wrong. Besides she had seen the fairy's corpse hung on a spider's web and the trail of blood in the dark.

She tried not to listen to the low cross adult voices until Ma said, "I'll speak to Madena."

Ma stood and smoothed her pants. Her face was flushed. Madena couldn't figure out if Ma was angry, as she helped Beca pack her crayons.

"Look at my frog. It slides down the rainbow to the pot of gold!" Beca stepped in front of Ms. Jefferson and Mr. Davis to show them.

Ms. Jefferson gave her a pinched smile and a nod. "It's a good frog, Rebeca."

"I am in pre-school. Then I got kindergarten, then first grade, then I'll be here, too."

"Won't that be nice," Mr. Davis replied. "We look forward to seeing you."

A surge of jealousy ripped through Madena's heart. Frogs don't really slide down spiraling rainbow bridges, yet her teachers didn't tell Beca not to draw those things. Obviously, Ms. Jefferson and Mr. Davis liked Beca better. They liked everyone better, because Madena was marbles-free.

"Thank you for bringing this to my attention. Come on, girls.

Let's get home."

"Ice cream, ice cream!" Beca shouted and hopped.

Ma clasped Beca's hand and hurried through the door. Madena slunk out behind them. At the car, Ma muttered in Spanish as she buckled Beca into her car seat. Madena wondered if she might be in trouble, but as she climbed in her booster seat, Ma flipped on her playlist of children's songs. She drove without speaking since Beca was singing. Beca was always singing.

"Don't become seven. You can't like pink, and you don't sing at school," Madena whispered under the song.

Beca didn't hear her.

At home, Ma set down her purse, then kicked off her shoes. She walked into the kitchen and scooped up three small bowls of ice cream. She handed Beca a bowl.

"I need to talk to Madi. Go play in the backyard."

This was it. Madena was in trouble now. The ice cream felt bitter in her mouth. She hated Second Grade Advanced Learning Opportunities.

Ma waited until they heard Beca babbling to herself, before she began a lecture. She spoke about how mamas and papies who love each other play private grown-up games and "It's impolite to talk about it."

Madena had no idea what Ma was talking about. She clenched her fists upon her lap. "My story was not about you and Papi playing a game. They say write about feelings, so I wrote about how Lobo's whining makes me sad."

Ma's eyes sparkled as she held in a chuckle. "Well, I liked your unicorn story better," she said.

"Ms. Jefferson and Mr. Davis didn't. Am I in trouble?"

"No."

"Can I go outside?"

"Yes," Ma replied and leaned down to kiss her brow, but Madena pulled away.

"I don't feel like a kiss now."

A momentary spot of hurt formed on her mother's face, but it disappeared quickly. "Well, mamita, when you feel like a kiss, I'll give you one."

Madena shuffled her feet against the cold vinyl flooring, across the rough mat to the backyard.

"Wanna play, Madi?"

Beca tried to push a Barbie whose legs were sticky with ice cream into Madena's hands, but she walked deeper into their mother's garden. She got on her belly and crawled underneath the rose bushes, where the thorns scratched her arms and Beca would not dare follow. This was where the heavy darkness lived. Ma called it *El Portal*. Papi said it was where the fairies crossed into our universe. Papi was glad science was finally catching up with what people knew for centuries. Fairies lived in another dimension. That's why nobody aged in fairyland.

"Don't turn seven," she whispered, though she knew Beca couldn't hear her.

Lying on the tilled earth, Madena felt the dampness of coming winter. The sunlight stenciled icy leaf shadows upon her skin. She closed her eyes and listened to the breeze shift the leaves above her.

When she opened her eyes again, she spied a fairy asleep on a branch.

As quietly as she could, she slipped from under the rosebush. Madena grabbed a plastic cup from the sandbox before her sister even turned around.

She scooped up the fairy. Wings beat the side of the cup. Tiny fingers pressed against the palm of her hand. A slicing pain as the fairy pinched and ripped out a tiny piece of flesh. She felt the blood rise to the surface, but did not flinch.

Raced towards the porch, she found the discarded glass gallon jar, once used as a fish tank until the fish was flushed. The fairy tumbled to the bottom before it caught its breath and flew towards the opening. Madena pushed the plastic cup onto the top and held it tight against the fury of the little beast.

She had to be careful. She could not allow her mother to see she captured a fairy. Ma and Papi wouldn't understand. Beca would tell. She glanced inside. Ma danced and sang off-key with the music as she vacuumed. Lobo Loco hated the vacuum, but loved it when Ma danced. He twirled and barked with sheer adulation at her feet.

Madena tore off a long piece of milkweed from the bush. The fairy dodged the hairy stem of faded orange blossoms and spiraling lanceolate leaves as it settled on the bottom of the jar. As she set a tiny saucer of water inside, the fairy scratched and bit her, but Madena did not care.

Trying to control her excitement, she slipped through the back door. She opened the third kitchen drawer and cut off a large square of cheesecloth and bit of twine. Pinching her lips together, she tied the twine around the fabric and jar as tight as she could with a double knot. Now the fairy had everything it needed, but it couldn't escape. She carried the jar to her room and set it upon her dresser where she could admire her prize.

Black veins surrounded sparkling orange scale-covered patches and a series of small white spots on fluttering wings. It was naked, but so much hair obscured its body, Madena could not tell if it was a boy or a girl. Maybe it didn't matter if you were a fairy.

"You're lucky to not have marketed gender roles," she whispered.

Ignoring her, it pushed up on the cheesecloth and tore at the loose strands, but the threads were too strong to give. It tossed a pebble, but the pebble just bounced off the heavy glass. Its tiny nails broke and trails of blood lined the jar, before it lay on the rocks panting. Its wings fluttered like mad.

"I want a wish," Madena said.

The fairy lifted its head. "I wish to be let go." Its high-pitched voice chirped in a panicked staccato.

"No. Give me a wish," Madena said. "I'll let you go if you give me a wish."

"I don't grant wishes."

"If you can't grant wishes, what are you good for?"

"I pollinate flowers and teach bees to dance. What are *you* good for?"

Madena did not realize the fairy's wings had begun to slow. "I want a unicorn and I want to know magic."

"Unicorns can't live in the suburbs and magic is all that which cannot be explained. Free me, I'm dying!" Its wings stopped thrashing and held perfectly still, but its chest heaved in rapid breaths.

"Get me out of school and I will let you go!"

"Look to your mother. She knows magic that I do not," the fairy said.

"Like what?" Madena hoped Ma really did know magic.

"She commands machines that clean and provide her family with heat and food," it said.

"That's not magic!"

"She pushes a button and music fills the house. Let me out. A fairy can't live confined!" It pounded its fists upon the glass.

"That's just the playlist on her phone!"

Madena smacked the side of the jar. The fairy covered its head with its arms and cried upon the rocks. She stormed out of her room and into the hallway and sat on the stairs.

Her mother was still dancing.

Madena liked the song, but she rolled her eyes and shouted, "Ma, you're embarrassing me!"

Her mother's face betrayed she was trying to figure out if she should be angry or concerned. "What?"

"Stop dancing!"

Lobo Loco whined.

Ma chose to be concerned. "Why don't you dance with me, mamita?"

Madena screamed, "Stop calling me that!"

Concern was eaten up by annoyance. Lobo Loco whimpered as Ma snatched her by the arm and pushed her into the too-small time-out chair.

Ten minutes to think about what she did wrong. Madena didn't care.

What hurt was afterwards.

Ma leaned over her and brushed a soft hand over her hair. Lobo Loco began licking Madena's hand. Ma touched her chin. "Want to talk about it? Still upset about your writing assignment?"

Madena shook her head, then nodded. Guilt slid into her heart and hot tears dripped out of her eyes.

"If you want to write about fairies or unicorns, you should. The point of free writing is to write about whatever you want. And if it is not, then it should be."

"What if I get an F?"

Ma looked a little concerned at the thought of an F, but she answered, "As long as you do the best you can, Papi and I'll be proud of you."

Warmth spread through Madena's chest. Maybe the fairy was right and there was magic in the house.

Madena climbed the stairs to her room. Something felt wrong in the darkness. She flipped on the light. Everything was where it ought to be, yet the fairy wasn't moving anymore. She pulled off the cheesecloth and pushed on the fairy's chest. It didn't move. Its bright orange wings faded. Ten tiny finger-trails of blood were visible on the glass.

"Wake up," she whispered.

Madena remembered the way to save fairies from Peter Pan. He made all the children clap to save Tinker Bell—even though it was night and their mothers would hear them. She clapped until her hands ached. The fairy did not even raise its head. She picked it up and set it by the window. It still didn't move.

She flicked it gently towards the end of the sill. It did not fly off. It just lay there. She flicked at it again. It was supposed to take wing and fly, but it just tumbled into the rosebush below.

"I didn't kill a fairy. I wouldn't have done that."

If she killed a fairy, there really was no magic, no unicorns, not even Santa Claus.

"It was just a butterfly, already at the end of its life," she whispered, not believing it. "Maybe it's just sick. Maybe it isn't dead?"

She ran outside to see if the fairy had revived under the rose bushes, but it just lay on the ground. Unmoving. Maybe she could give it a funeral.

No, she couldn't. Ma might see. She would get in trouble. She slid it into her jacket pocket. She sniffed.

Feeling its lifeless form, she whispered, "It might be a toy. It might be a butterfly. No one has to know."

Madena wiped the bit of snot from her nose. She had proof fairies existed. Maybe she should show the girls in her class. They wouldn't laugh and push her anymore. Maybe she could show Mr. Davis. Then he would know she could write brave. She turned towards her house. A bright flash, and the house disappeared.

Madena could only see fluttering wings reflecting the afternoon sunlight into her eyes. She put her arms in front of her face and took a step back. Small hands struck her torso, arms, and legs. To release the pressure, she took another step. They pushed her into the rose bushes. She fell onto the dirt. Thorns snagged on her hair, bare hands and jacket.

"Mama!" she cried.

A fairy landed in front of her face. She tried to bat it away, but it flew too quickly. "You didn't want to go back to second grade. You won't."

From the porch, she heard Beca scream.

Madena felt herself moved toward the gateway by the force of the fairies' wings. She screamed and clawed at the dirt. Earth filled her fingernails and scraped her elbows. She grabbed upon a thorny cane of her mother's rose bush. The thorns pressed into her scraped palms. Drops of blood slid onto the ground.

Her legs felt heavier as she was dragged downward, energy pressed into her lower body. They seemed to stretch and elongate. Sweat beaded on her forehead as she tried to clamber away from the portal.

She screamed again, "Mama!"

"Madena!"

Trying to break through the wall of fluttering wings, Ma's hands reached towards her. "Don't hurt my baby! Madi!"

The fairies pried open Madena's fingers and licked the blood from them. One whispered, "No school, no books…"

Another whispered, "No Mama's kisses, either." And pulled her middle finger from the cane.

Madena's last finger slipped. She tried to hold on, but pain seared her flesh as the slippery cane and thorns slashed her hands.

"Nothing you don't want. All your dreams are about to come true," a fairy said. "You will be an eternal child in our world."

The gateway swallowed her. Air hitched in her raw throat as Madena slid into the darkness. Her only conscious thought was that she was elongating. That's what happened when someone was pushed into a portal. She would stretch until she snapped into a million pieces.

Or perhaps not. Mama and Papi had never told her what was on the other side, only that it was fairyland.

~ * ~ * ~

Elizabeth Guizzetti is an illustrator, podcaster, and the author of *Accident Among Vampires or What Would Dracula Do?* and many other novels, short stories, and comics. Guizzetti resides in Seattle with her husband and their dog. When not writing or illustrating, she loves hiking and birdwatching.

Find out more on Instagram (@elizabeth_guizzetti) and Facebook (Elizabeth.Guizzetti.Author)

ᚨhe ᚠᚨᚱmeᚱ ᚨnᚨ ᚨhe ᚠᚨiᚱy

An Indonesian folk tale
adapted by James Penha

In this time, we have accustomed ourselves to the nudity of sprites and nymphs. Indeed, thanks to the impressions of artists (and a few truly rude pornographers), we can stare at fleshy buds just where we, bound by our human nature, wish to see them on the serene bodies of fairies and elves. Yet even as we remember that pixies and their like share a corporeal reality with us, we have forgotten some things. In the olden days, fairies depended for flight not on wings, but on magical robes.

It was in those times that six of the most beautiful fairies spoke together in their great magic kingdom in the clouds. Three were male, and three were female, and all wished to feel the pleasure of a dawn swim in Lake Toba, on the great island of Sumatra. They donned their gowns to fly to earth. Once safely descended, the fairies disrobed, threw their gowns along the lakeside, and dove into Toba's stirring coolness.

Now none of this escaped the notice of a young Batak farmer. The farmer had set out early, hoping to earn a few rupiah by selling a sack of small potatoes. Instead, he earned the sight of beauty rarely beheld by humans of any tribe. Such perfection to the eye would have satisfied most of us, I think. We would have continued our work with a sense of wonder.

But the farmer was young and unconcerned with the knowledge of boundaries. He wanted a fairy. He would have taken any one of them, but he considered future success as well as present appetites and chose a sweet, golden female. As the fairies swam deep in Lake Toba, the farmer found sweet Angela's gown. He rolled it tightly and stuffed it into the loincloth under his sarong.

When the fairies felt the lake grow warm with daylight, they swam to shore and gathered their clothes for the flight back to the clouds. Even as the other five rose past the treetops, Angela searched for her gown. She called to her friends for help, but not even fairies can see the truth hidden in the underwear of a selfish man.

Angela lifted her voice. "I know now that I must stay. Return and tell my parents in the clouds that I shall live as good a life as I can on Earth, for as long as I remain bound to the ground."

When the five fairies had become less than dust to human eyes, the young Batak farmer approached the lonely beauty. He feigned surprise at finding a young woman in such a natural state.

"Are you mad? It is not safe to walk naked here," he said.

"Tell me what I do not already know. Already I have lost everything!" Angela spoke without shame. She stared at the farmer directly, her arms outstretched.

The farmer removed his sarong and draped it around Angela. "Who are you?" he asked, though silently he gloated, *"I know who you are!"*

"I am one who is in your debt," she said. "Especially since your favor has left you looking foolish in a lumpy loincloth."

"The world will find me foolish to offer you all I have. But, if you accept, humble though my life may be, I shall count myself among the wisest of men."

Angela followed the farmer. She became his wife, the mother of his children, and mistress of an ever more prosperous plantation. Adored and pampered by her husband, Angela was satisfied as much as any earthly woman could hope for in those days. The farmer knew how fortunate he was to have married a fairy. He kept the secret of her gown hidden in his tool shed, in a clay urn, which became more and more humble in comparison to his more and more elegant home.

In all other ways, in life and business, the farmer sought to be worthy of his fairy wife. His neighbors came to revere the farmer for his honesty and charity. As his sons grew older, the farmer taught them the operation of the plantation so that they, in turn, might achieve greater success.

It happened that Muchtar, the son to whom the father had given the business of the lambs, discovered an illness among a number of his flock. Instead of destroying the entire flock, as his father would have done in the past, Muchtar cremated only the sickly-looking lambs. The rest he sheared and slaughtered for stew meat to sell at the market.

By nightfall of the market day, seven families burned with fever and ached with diarrhea. The village chief confronted the farmer with the apparent effect of his son's meat. Appalled, the farmer demanded Muchtar defend his product. The sheepish son could only tell the truth.

"How could the son of a fairy do such evil?" screamed the farmer. "May you be punished by all that is divine. Get away from me. You might have killed someone!"

Muchtar sought comfort in the drawing room of his mother. He told her all, from his own foolish decision to his father's strange and angry words.

"Your father will forgive you, my child, but you must learn from your mistakes. Leave me now, for I have a long-neglected chore to complete this day."

Alone, Angela sat to catch her breath. "He knows who I am. He knows I am a fairy. He has always known!"

She repeated these words, ever more quickly and loudly, until her keening voice cracked every glass and vase in the drawing room. She rose and sang the same dirge in every room. Wooden chests buckled. Every piece of clay, china or ceramic broke into bits. Angela even dared to enter her husband's tool shed and make it her auditorium. There she shrieked the farmer's old clay urn into dust. In the rubble she saw her gown, unworn for twenty years.

She knelt before it. Her hands spread wide the fabric's fine pattern. Angela tore off all the rich garments her husband had draped upon her. She easily donned the gown he had hidden. Angela left the tool shed and the house, all the fragments of her life on Earth. From a knoll in the farmer's fields, she leapt, flew, and returned to the clouds.

~ * ~ * ~

Expat New Yorker **James Penha** has lived for the past three decades in Indonesia. Nominated for Pushcart Prizes in fiction and poetry, his work is widely published in journals and anthologies. His newest chapbook of poems, *American Daguerreotypes*, is available for Kindle. Penha edits The New Verse News, an online journal of current-events poetry. Twitter: @JamesPenha Threads: @PenhaJames

Che Oullahan's Coach

Samuel Poots

Spare some change, mate?"

The business man deftly stepped around Tom's outstretched hand, not even breaking stride. Tom sighed and leant back against the cold brick of the wall, drawing his sleeping bag up around him. The street by the book shop didn't get much foot traffic. There were better chances of a handout just one lane away. On the other side of a single row of buildings, Belfast citizens hustled their way through the wide main street, cutting into the Castle Court shopping centre or one of the big name stores that framed the road like high class sentinels.

Of course, more people didn't necessarily mean more money was going to come your way. Tom had learnt that his first year on the streets. You became just part of the architecture, an inescapable feature of the street to be stepped around as you avoided eye contact with your fellow members of the crowd. Plus, there were buskers and store security and the like, who didn't want you intruding on their stretch and were likely to hustle you along before you could pick up much. So better to stay in the side streets.

"Gettin' no luck today, Tom?"

He looked up and was greeted by the sight of a mug of steaming tea. "Aye, thanks, Bill." He took the proffered cup.

The old book shop owner smiled and pushed his glasses up the bridge of his nose. "Don't mention it. You get much today?"

Tom sorted through the change in his polystyrene cup. "Er, couple of quid, I think. Not too bad, I suppose." He shot the man a quick grin from behind his beard. "Enough to buy a book from you, eh?"

"Ha, don't taunt me," Bill said, leaning against the door frame to his shop. "The way I see it, you're doing almost better than I am these days."

"Want to change places?"

Bill scratched the white bristles of his chin for a moment. "Promise you'd take the missus, too?"

"Er, I'll pass."

The shop keeper chuckled and took a long swig from his own mug. A pair of high school age kids went past, still in their uniforms. Surreptitious cigarettes hung from their lips. Tom didn't even bother asking for change. For some reason, people were less inclined to take notice if you were enjoying a cuppa.

"They don't mean to neglect you, you know," Bill said softly.

"What's that?"

"People." The old man nodded after the kids, who had turned the corner back toward the centre of town. "It isn't because they don't care that they don't notice."

Tom grunted. "What's it matter why? Doesn't help me get a sandwich, does it?"

"Aye, well," Bill shrugged. "To them I expect you're just another face in a sea of faces they can't really help."

Tom drained the last of his tea, wincing as the hot liquid burned down his gullet. "You put a bit of brandy in that, didn't you?"

The old man winked, his glasses magnifying the gesture, and drained the rest of his own mug. "Where're you sleeping these days, Tom?"

"If I'm there quick enough, I can usually get myself some kip at the Welcome."

"You mean that homeless shelter down Townsend?"

"Aye." Tom reached over and checked Bill's wristwatch. "Should be able to make it if I move soon."

"Hmm." Bill stared off into the middle distance. His mouth moved, like he was trying to dislodge some annoying bit of food wedged in his teeth, a habit Tom had noticed whenever he was coming to a decision. "Look, why don't you bunk down in the shop tonight? You can roll out your sleeping bag behind the counter and I'll get a few pillows or something to make you a bed."

Tom smiled at the old man and got to his feet, gathering the sleeping bag about him. "Thanks, but I wouldn't put you to the trouble."

"Oh, it's no trouble," Bill said, giving Tom a sly smile of his own. "Trust me, you'd be doing me a favour." He pointed at a large crack that cobwebbed the store's window. "Some ruffians were here last night. Gave me and my wife an awful shock with their racket. I come down this morning to find this. If you were to hang about here tonight, maybe catch the wee bastards in the act, I could see to it you get a little pay. How about it?"

Tom eyed the warm interior of the book shop. Even from outside he could smell the comforting scent of old, dry paper. "You sure it wouldn't be too much of a hassle?"

"Not at all. Just don't make too much noise, if you can. The missus and I are in the room right above the store entrance and she'd give me a right earful if she was kept up the night."

"Well, all right, if you insist. But—"

"But me no buts." Bill plucked the mug from Tom's hands and turned back into his shop. "Come on, we can see about getting you something to eat."

~ * ~

It was warm enough in the book shop. Tom lay back on the old army-style cot Bill had set up for him behind a counter. Upstairs he could just make out the murmur of conversation between Bill and his wife as they prepared for bed. As Bill had predicted, Maggie had made a bit of a fuss about him staying the night under their roof. But she had given him dinner and even a second helping without him asking for it.

Outside, heavy drops of rain began to spatter against the windows. A wind picked up, rattling the metal grille Bill had drawn down to cover the store front. Inside, though, all was warmth. A small desk light spilled its orange glow around the dark store and the smell of books filled Tom's nostrils. He scanned a couple of the bookshelves for anything interesting.

The old shopkeeper had tried to keep things fairly organized, with shelving devoted to each genre. However, the books had piled up over the years and people just weren't buying them quickly enough. The end result was that, instead of books being neatly filed into their respective slots, they had spilled out of their shelves like water from a burst pipe. Stacks of books tottered everywhere like literary stalactites. It all gave the impression that the books weren't exactly organized, but instead gravitated to their allocated area of the store.

Tom reached out and picked up a book at random. The title read *Irish Fairy and Folk Tales, edited and selected by W. B. Yeats*. Like most kids growing up on the island of Ireland, he had been subjected to the Irish poet's work. He lay back on the cot and, as the rain began to thunder down against the glass, he read. That night, the fairies and heroes of old Ireland danced once again under his eyes. He found some peace there, for peace comes dropping slow. Sleep, however, dropped less slowly, and Tom soon found his eyes begin to droop.

The shop's metal grating shot up. Tom started at the loud crash, struggling free of his sleeping bag.

Lock must have come loose, he thought.

But no, he had watched Bill lock the place up. The padlock holding the grating down had looked sturdy enough. Then he saw a shape pass in front of the rain-smeared windows.

Tom smiled and reached down for the old golf club Bill had left behind the counter. That hellion who smashed the window. God only knew why he had chosen to continue his torment tonight. The black form moved slowly towards the shop's door. Tom ducked down under the window ledge and reached out for the door handle. He felt the beard on his face to make sure it was suitably tangled and adopted a crooked, evil grin. This little tit was going to have the fright of his life. The silhouette appeared in the window of the door, outlined by the barely perceptible glow of a streetlamp across the road.

Tom slammed back the door, golf club in hand and glared down at the figure. "All right you little twat, let's see your—Mary Mother of Mercy!"

A man stood there, slightly shorter than him and dressed in the faded black clothes of a period drama. The rain drenched him, making the old fashioned cloak stick to his body and flattening the high collar framing the space where his head should have been.

The club clattered to the ground. Tom stared at the shadowed darkness where a face normally looked back. He felt his throat freeze and his knees weaken. A voice came from the empty air.

"William O'Donnell?"

Tom could see the streetlamp on the other side of the road. From where he stood, it appeared to be jutting out of the figure's neck. "Er, what?"

"Are you William O'Donnell?"

"Er, no. Tom Farrell." The rain splashed into Tom's face, cold water hitting him like pricks of ice. He shook the shock out of his mind and looked over the figure critically. "Very good. You get that from one of the ghost tours did you?"

The headless figure didn't answer. Tom knelt down and investigated the buttonholes of the 'spectre's' shirt.

"See out of one of these, right?" He smiled and shook his head. "I have to say, A for effort, lad, but this is really sad, trying to scare an old man like that." He retrieved the golf club and stood, stretching up to his full height. "Now, you just head on, and I won't be forced to—"

There was a loud whinny down the street. Tom turned and came face to face with a black horse. Or he would have, if the horse hadn't been missing its head as well. It stood in the middle of the narrow road, hitched up to a grand, black carriage. As far as Tom could tell, it seemed to act as any other horse would. It shook itself in the rain, tail swishing restlessly. It just happened not to have a head.

"I am here for William O'Donnell." The headless man stepped closer. He began unwrapping a white length of whip from around one arm. It took Tom a second to recognize it as being made from segments of human spine. He tightened his grip on the golf club.

"Who… What are you?"

The empty darkness above the collar regarded the homeless man. Then its voice once again emerged from thin air in a whisper that carried louder than the hammering rain. "I am Dullahan."

Tom gulped. "Oh, hell." He knew the name. He had read it just a few hours past. Dullahan, the headless fairy riders of Ireland who came to claim the souls of the dying. "You're not real." He found himself saying, shaking his head. "You're just something out of *Derby O'Gill.*"

The headless man ignored him. It stepped past the stunned Tom and into the shop.

"I am not here for you," it said.

The sight of the spectre making its way to the back of the store snapped Tom out of his stupor. That thing was here for Bill. Bill had been kind. He hadn't needed to, but he had invited Tom into his home. His goddamned home! Now this…this storybook monster was here to take even that! A smile tugged the corner of his lips. No matter what vandals or horrors from the old days of Éire, he had been trusted with protecting the shop and that was what he was going to do.

The Dullahan came up short as Tom's heavy hand landed on its collar. "Look you," Tom said, raising the club threateningly. "You go get up on your headless horse and get the hell out of here."

"I am not here for you." The voice sounded again, but this time there seemed to be an edge of confusion to it.

"Aye, well I ain't about to stand by." He put all his strength behind the blow, the iron club whistling as it came around.

What happened next went too fast for Tom to follow. One minute he was there, holding the Dullahan back and preparing to bring the club down across its shoulders. The next, he was flying fast out of the shop door. He came to a crash on the slick brick paving of the alley. His arm felt numb, his fingers tingled. The Dullahan stood in the doorway of the shop, a golf club twisted and bent in one hand.

"You will not stop me from claiming him!" This time the voice was like thunder and Tom had to cover his ears at the force of it. The remains of the club clanged as it too was flung from the shop. Then the headless horseman turned and walked back into the store.

"No, wait! Come back here!"

The sinister fey didn't turn. Tom tried to pick himself up, but his arm gave way under him and he splashed back down into a puddle. It was going to kill him. The thought screamed in his head. A creature out of nightmares was going to kill his friend. He made another try and this time managed to stand, on legs that felt weak and shaky beneath him. He had to do something. His mind flashed to all those people who had walked past him over the years, who had ignored him and stepped around him. Bill hadn't. Bill had done something. Now here Tom was, completely helpless to return the favour.

He looked around, trying to find someone he could call for help —a policeman, a traffic warden, a God damned milk man would have done! Then his eyes fell on something and an idea began to form in his mind. It was a stupid idea, one that would definitely get him killed.

"What the hell." He said, clambering up to the driver's box of the black coach. "We all die anyway."

The reins cracked loudly. The headless horse reared up in a whinny, then the coach surged forward, its wheels bouncing across the street.

Even over all that noise, Tom managed to hear the yell from inside the shop. He looked back over his shoulder to see the Dullahan rush out of the front door.

"Ha! How'd you like that, you bastard?" He shouted back at the black figure. "Can't take anyone anywhere without this, can you? Oh shit!" Tom turned back and clung to the reins for dear life as the headless horse swerved the carriage out round and onto Royal Avenue, heading fast toward the City Hall.

There was no traffic at this time of night. Shuttered shop fronts shot past as Tom, screaming at the top of his lungs, rattled through the dark streets of Belfast on a stolen fairy carriage. Lack of a head didn't seem to bother the horse at all. It sped on, ducking down alleys and streets, apparently oblivious to the weight of the black coach behind it. As far as Tom could tell, the horse was just taking turns randomly, which was just as well considering he didn't know how to steer a coach, let alone a headless horse.

Then, to his great surprise, a voice called out from behind him. "Oi, what's going on? Why are we going so feckin' fast?"

For a moment, he was sure the horse had spoken. After all, hadn't the Dullahan coachman's voice come out of thin air like that?

"Hey, you boy, I'm talkin' to you here. You deaf, or what?"

"Er… I'm sorry to steal you like this," Tom said, staring at the horse. "But I just really wanted to help my friend."

Something tapped him on the arm. He jumped and almost dropped the reins. Turning, he found himself addressed by a red-faced man hanging out one of the coach windows.

"If you stole this, boy, I think you're going to find yourself in more shit than you can swim in." He said, glaring up at Tom.

Tom gaped at the man in wide-mouthed surprise. "What are you doing in there?!"

"I'm doing the feckin' crossword, what do you think?" The man turned the ferocity of his glare up a notch.

"What's happening out there?" Came a querulous old voice from inside.

The red-faced man turned back to the other occupant. "Some lad's gone and stolen the coach, love."

"What's he done that for?"

"Search me." The man returned to glaring at Tom. "Well? Let's hear some explanation."

"Are you dead?" Tom asked.

The man was about to answer when the coach went over a pothole. He smacked his head on the window frame and ducked back into the coach, a steady stream of curses pouring from his mouth. This meant Tom's view back was no longer obstructed, letting him see the Dullahan following in hot pursuit.

The headless man was running down the centre of the road in great, loping strides that ate up the distance. It didn't even look to be moving that fast, its movements slow and graceful. Yet Tom could see it was definitely catching up, its black cloak billowing about it as it ran. For some reason, the sight put Tom in mind of the old Scooby-Doo cartoons that used to be on. The characters would be running in the centre of the screen, but when you watched carefully you saw it was the background moving, not them.

The red-faced man stuck his head out of the window again, apparently ready to give Tom an earful, but stopped when he saw Tom's face. He turned and caught sight of the pursuing Dullahan.

"Oh shit, lad," he said, turning a look of sympathy on Tom. "We may be dead, but I think it might be a tad worse for you if that one catches you, eh?"

Tom nodded mutely and returned to the box. When he looked back, he could see the Dullahan only a few yards behind. He cracked the reins and the horse seemed to find an extra reserve of speed from somewhere. The coach lurched and there was once again a chorus of swearing from inside the cab.

"I do wish you wouldn't swear like that," said the querulous old voice. "It was bad enough having to put up with such manners in life."

Still the Dullahan came on. They had hit a straight, with no turns other than narrow alleys on either side. As Tom watched, it reached out with a gloved hand and grasped a rail on the side of the door. Even without a face, Tom could feel its attention on him. He yanked hard on the reins. The headless horse swerved hard to the left. The coach skidded round and headed down one of the alleys. The Dullahan was caught off guard and flung wide, right into a wall. Tom thought he heard an oomph of pain before the horseman dropped out of sight.

He cracked the reins again for good measure. The sides of the coach scraped along the narrow walls of the alley, setting up a screech like a dying animal. His chest felt tight and his breathing ragged. Cold sweat dripped from his forehead and down the tip of his nose, mixing with the driving rain hitting him in the face. For a while he lost track of where they were. Turn blurred into turn, road into road. It became a stream of never-ending motion, the darkened windows of the sleeping city zipping past. Behind him, he was vaguely aware of a conversation going on in the carriage.

"What'll this mean? Reckon they'll still let us in?"

"In where, love?"

"Wherever we're headed, of course. I mean, do we get points off for turning up late?"

"Don't you worry, I've been a loyal member of Ballysillan Presbyterian. Every Sunday, regular as clockwork. You mark my words, love, we'll be all right."

"Hm." From the sound of it, the old lady didn't take regular church attendance as something entirely reassuring. "But what about this lad? He's gone and stolen the coach. My father used to tell me stories about the Dullahan when I was a wee'un. Fairies who didn't belong to any court are the most dangerous, he said. These ones would whip your eyes out if you caught sight of them before your time, he said. I'd hate for the young man to end up like that."

"Aye, well can't be helped. He was the one daft enough to steal the coach, eh? 'Ere, hang on, we're slowing."

Tom's attention came back to the here and now with a snap. Sure enough, their pace was rapidly faltering. He looked at the horse and saw its sides heaving with exhaustion. Quite how a headless horse could pant, he didn't know. Yet it was definitely in distress. In his peripheral vision, he fancied he caught a glimpse of a flapping black cloak.

"Hyah!" He shouted, cracking the reins again. "Come on, gee up. Mush. Get goin', ye bastard."

The creature didn't react. It just kept slowing its pace until eventually they ground to a halt.

"Oh, are we here, then, dear?" Came the querulous voice of the old lady inside.

"Aye? And where is here exactly?" The red-faced man stuck his head out the window again. His face fell. "Oh God." His face managed to turn an even darker shade of crimson. "He's only gone and taken us to the feckin' Falls Road."

"Ooh, lovely. My Gracie lives around here. I wonder if I'll be allowed to say cheerio before I head off to wherever it is."

Tom looked around the street. The rain had begun to ease off at last. Nationalist flags and banners hung limply from lamp posts. He clambered down from the box, keeping a watchful eye out for any sign of the Dullahan. He doubted that meeting with the wall would have slowed it down for long. The horse was worn out. Its sides heaved and its legs shook beneath it. Tom patted its flank absently. At the very least, he'd succeeded in getting them as far from Bill's as he could. He walked over and opened the door to the carriage. Inside sat a small old woman with tightly curled grey hair, across from the red-faced man who Tom could now see was built like an out-of-shape gorilla. Both of them were wearing their pajamas, although neither seemed to be particularly uncomfortable about this.

"Well?" The red-faced man demanded. "What's it you want?"

Tom opened his mouth to answer. Then he shut it again. What was he going to do now? He hadn't exactly planned to steal the thing's coach. Somehow he doubted that was going to make it any easier on him when it caught up.

"Go on," he said at last. "Get out of here."

"What's that, dear?" The old lady smiled gently.

"Get out of here. The Dullahan is most likely going to be after me. I know my way around the city well enough. I'll leg it. If you two leave now it probably won't catch you."

Two quizzical looks met him from the coach, one distinctly kinder than the other.

"Why'd we want to run, love?"

"Aye, no way I'm gettin' out at the feckin' Falls." The red-face man crossed his arms like a hairy barrier against all things Republican.

Tom gaped at them. "Do you want to die?"

"Not especially," the old lady conceded.

"Then why stay? You could be out and away, carrying on with your lives. The Dullahan wouldn't carry you off."

The man grunted. "Maybe that's right. Most like not. But it ain't about wanting. We're dead. It's our time. No point in wailin' up a storm about it."

"You can't be serious!" Tom shouted, his voice echoing down the silent street. "You're just going to lie back and do nothing?" He waved his finger under the nose of the red-faced man, who looked so shocked that he managed a slightly paler shade for once. "I live on the street. I have no one. Not one person. Yet if you think I'd just let that thing carry you off, let alone the one person who has shown me a bit of kindness lately, you've got another think coming."

Tom panted as rage burst from long-blocked dams. It was a rage that came from years of being ignored, of being stepped around and treated like the gum that stuck to the pavement. It came from those who had run him off when he had tried to sleep in their shop fronts, from when city workers had put spikes wherever he could sleep with some degree of comfort. It was a white-hot rage, fuelled by neglect and sparked by his own impotence when he finally had a chance to show them he cared enough to do something.

He shouted. He didn't know what. Words were flung from his mouth at the two occupants of the coach. He swore and raged and yelled until finally he had to stop, his voice horse and hurting. Inside the coach, the red-faced man had backed away as far from Tom as he could. The old lady still sat perfectly still with her pleasant half-smile, although it seemed rather more fixed than it had before. Somewhere, a dog started barking.

"I'm not going to stand by," Tom said, his voice a whisper now. "You two can stay if you want. Go or stay, I ain't letting that bastard take anyone."

The red-faced man gulped, radiating nervousness. "Well pal, now's your chance to tell him so yourself."

Tom turned. Standing a mere arm's length from him was the Dullahan. It looked none the worse for having been flung into a wall. Its macabre whip hung down from one gloved hands, the bone sections clicking lightly as a breeze stirred the night air.

The homeless man's shoulders drooped. It took all his strength not to simply fall to the floor.

"You know what?" he said, addressing the Dullahan directly. "I know this is pointless. I know Bill will…will die one day anyway. And I know you're probably going to whip my eyes out for this." He looked at the whip and a quaver entered his voice. "But I don't care. You hear me?"

Tom straightened up to his full height and backed away until he blocked the door of the carriage, arms stretched out to either side. "It won't be tonight. Tonight I can do something, you hear? You hear me, you Sleepy Hollow bastard?!"

The horseman lifted one gloved hand and pointed into the carriage. "What of these two? These are not who you are trying to save."

"They are. They all are! It makes no difference. Least I'm keeping them out of your hands." He closed his eyes and let his head droop to his chest. "All right, do your worst."

He flinched as he heard the clack of bones. In his mind's eye he saw the whip, raised up over the sepulchral creature's shoulder, ready to flick out and pluck his eyes from his skull.

The carriage shook gently behind him and he heard the door on the other side open. "All right, that's quite enough of that now."

He opened his eyes in shock to find the old lady striding purposefully out from behind the coach towards the Dullahan, which did indeed have its whip raised. Behind her, the large figure of the red-faced man followed, showing rather more unease than the grey-haired woman. The lady walked up to Dullahan and prodded it purposefully in the chest.

"What do you think you are doing, eh?" Though the rider was small, it still managed to tower over the irate octogenarian, who glared up at where its head should be, two bright blue eyes twinkling furiously behind wire-rimmed spectacles.

The whip didn't move. "He stole the coach," the Dullahan's sourceless voice echoed. "He attempted to prevent passage to the afterlife. Had he succeeded, you might have become mindless sluagh, driven by hunger and torment upon the West winds."

"Oh, and I suppose you've never made a mistake?" She said, prodding it again. "It was a bloody stupid thing to do, I agree, but he did it with good intentions. No need to go whipping his eyes out."

"Aye," the red-faced man said from behind the woman's shoulder. "Man's a bloody idiot, but no need for that, like."

The Dullahan turned from one to the other. Slowly, it let its whip drop. "What would you have me do with him, then?" Tom thought he detected a slight hint of amusement in the thing's tone.

"Let him be," the woman said.

"Shall he go unpunished?"

The woman nodded. "The lad wanted to help. Problem is he tried to help the wrong ones. He needs to go back and learn that."

Again, there was a long moment of drawn out silence, in which the only sound was the laboured breathing of the headless horse. Then, with a flick of his wrist, the whip wrapped back around the rider's arm like a living thing. The Dullahan pushed its way past the two and strode over to the coach. It stopped before it reached Tom and laid one hand upon the horse's flank.

"You have exhausted my steed." It said, completely deadpan.

Tom said nothing, afraid of anything that might persuade it to unwind its terrible whip once again.

It moved on to investigate the side of the coach, where it ran a gloved finger along the scratched paintwork. "You have ruined my coach."

It turned suddenly to face Tom, who flinched back in surprise. A sigh seemed to escape from wherever it was that its voice came from. "By all rights and laws of Fairy, I should not only blind you, but strip the sanity from you, too. I should leave you mad and bloody to walk the streets of this city." Its form seemed to grow larger and Tom shrank back before it. "You have dared to cross a rider of the fey. All would look upon you and know the folly of your actions, as you would be an outcast of men."

A savage smile forced its way onto Tom's face. "Go ahead," he whispered. "See what a difference it will make to my life."

Then the rider was normal sized again, the dark menace that had radiated from it dissipated. It continued as though Tom had never spoken. "As these two have said, you did so for laudable reasons. And, to be honest, it has been some time since a mortal last provided me with such entertainment. So, I will be lenient this time."

It took a step closer, and Tom could see the night seeming to swirl slightly above its shoulders. "I offer you this advice now. You cannot help those who are dead. They are beyond your reach. But there is still work for you to do."

Before Tom had a chance to react, it grasped his head in its rough leather gloves. He tried to struggle, but the grip was like a vice, which slackened only slightly as one hand disappeared into the folds of its cloak and came out holding a small cup. It held this above Tom's face and gently tipped it out. Blood poured out in a continuous stream. It fell upon his face and into his eyes. He tried to scream, but the warm, scarlet liquid filled his mouth. The blood made him gag and he felt himself retching.

Still the cup poured, and as it did Tom felt the world around him fade away. A crimson so dark as to be almost black crept into the sides of his vision. The last thing he saw was the headless shadow of the Dullahan.

~ * ~

"Tom. Tom, are you all right? Do I need to phone the ambulance?"

Tom managed to pry his eyelids open and was greeted by the worried face of Bill's wife.

"Do you need the doctor, love?" she asked.

Tom groaned and sat up. He was lying on the tiled floor of the book shop.

"I'm fine, Maggie," he said, remembering the woman's name. Behind him, the door swung open, pushed by the gentle morning breeze.

"Are you sure? You're covered in blood, man. One of the ruffians must have given you a fair whack, I expect."

Tom raised one hand to his head. His fingertips came away crimson. His mind's eye flashed back to the previous night. The headless Dullahan standing over him. The world turning crimson. Ice ran down his spine at the memory and he had to fight to not start shivering uncontrollably. The world had turned scarlet and now it was back to normal. He was back in a world with no room for the fey or headless horsemen. He could feel the night trying to slip away from him, like a dream. But then he looked down again at the blood on his fingers. No. No way had it been a dream.

Meanwhile Maggie fussed around him, probing his scalp with gentle fingers. "Well, I can't see anything the matter." She took off her spectacles and pinched the bridge of her nose. She'd got blood on her dressing gown, staining the floral pattern. Then she sat down on the foot of the cot Bill had set up and put her face in her hands. "Thank God for that. It would be the last thing we'd need today."

She looked up at Tom and her normally steel grey eyes looked clouded and confused. "Bill's dead Tom. He passed away in his sleep." Her voice started to crack and her shoulders shook. "I woke up this morning and there he was beside me. The most peaceful smile on him you ever did see."

Tears were running down the old woman's face now. Tom didn't know what to do. He didn't know what to say. He picked himself up off the floor and hung his head.

"I'm sorry, Maggie," he whispered. "I tried my best."

"Sorry? What have you to be sorry for, boy?" Maggie took in a few deep breaths, but still didn't look up at him.

Tom's whole body shook and he felt tears in the corners of his own eyes. "I tried," he sobbed. "I wanted to help, but I failed. And now there's nothing more to do."

A hand gripped his own. It was thin and wrinkled, but age couldn't hide the strength Maggie once had.

"Now you listen to me, Tom," she said, her voice under tight reign. "You should not be worrying yourself about those hellions. Not now. You did your best, lad, and near as I can tell you damn near killed yourself trying to help. No one can ask more of a body. But now there is more important stuff as needs doing."

She reached into a pocket of the dressing gown and drew out a handkerchief, carefully drying her eyes. "There." She gave him a weak smile. "My Bill always said as not to cry. Tears are for the living, he said. The dead don't need them. Now, you go get yourself cleaned up. I'll be needing some assistance, if you don't mind. Shower's first door on the left, upstairs."

It was a strange day after that. The doctor came soon after to see Bill. The old boy still lay in bed, looking for all the world like he had fallen asleep. Tom worked at keeping the place clean, dusting and hoovering while Maggie made calls. He learned from the doctor, as he made the lady a cup of tea, that Bill had been suffering from 'a long illness.' That abominable code people used when they were too afraid to say the daemon's name.

The news of Bill's death spread out slowly through the city, and as it did people started to come to the book shop where the old couple lived. Many brought casseroles and other such meals, and Maggie thanked them all kindly and piled the dishes up on the kitchen table. All wore the same expression; a kind of sorrowful determination, the look of people who know they can't make it better, but still want to do something. Tom watched them and thought back to the man and woman who had ridden with him through the Belfast streets.

All the while Maggie bore everything, the well-wishes and the condolences, the medical examinations and the phone calls, with a sort of stolid determination. It seemed to Tom that she went somewhere else behind her eyes each time and let her mouth do the talking. He worked hard at making sure all the food was safely stored and started to clean the kitchen. Maggie had assured him that this was only the start. More would be round in the week to come, and Tom knew the old woman would have been ashamed if her home was anything less than spotless, bereavement or no.

It felt as though night came far earlier that day, not long after the stream of people began to turn to a trickle. Once everyone had gone, Tom somehow found himself standing beside the bed where Bill lay. Maggie stood beside him, holding Bill's hand. There were no tears. She had cried all the tears she needed to that morning. Nonetheless, Tom could see a deeper sorrow there, one that went beyond tears and cries of mourning. It was loss, pure and simple. He took her gently by the arm. She started at his touch, and then smiled at him.

"He was a real pain in the backside sometimes, you know?" she said, looking Tom straight in the eye. "He had the learning to be a teacher, or what have you, but he wouldn't have left this shop for the world." She looked back down where Bill lay. "Daft old bugger." She let go of his hand and led Tom away.

"Thank you so much for helping out today, Mr. Farrell."

Tom shrugged. "Don't mention it. It really was the least I could do."

"Aye, well, still, you've been a big help is all I can say. Any idea when you plan to be moving on?"

"I'll be around as long as you need the help."

She gave his arm a gentle squeeze. "I'm… sorry, Tom." She said, as he helped her down the stairs. "I've never been all that kind to you, I don't think. You were always cluttering up the door. I told Bill that you'd scare off customers, but he'd have none of it."

Tom smiled at the thought of Bill calmly arguing for him. "Well, I can tell you, I'm not helping you just for Bill's sake."

"Oh? Why, then?"

In his head, Tom thought back over the events of the night and day. The carriage rattling through the rain-slicked streets. The dark coat billowing out from behind headless shoulders. Two people in their pajamas, staring down the horrific horseman. And this woman who had made sure he was uninjured, even in the face of grief.

"It took me a while to get it," he said at last. "Whatever we do, we can't help the dead. That doesn't mean the dead can't help the living sometimes, though. So that's what I'm doing. In memory."

Bill's widow looked at him, her head cocked to one side. Then she shrugged. "You don't half talk a load of ol' shite, Tom. Right, I'll get the kettle on."

~ * ~ * ~

Samuel Poots is a writer from N. Ireland who communicates primarily through Pratchett quotes. As a writer for TTRPGs, his work has been featured in Warhammer Fantasy RPG, Warhammer 40,000: Imperium Maledictum, and Jim Henson's Labyrinth: The Adventure Game, while his short stories have appeared in Daily Science Fiction, Dark Matter Magazine, and the Crunchy with Chocolate anthology. He is currently the writer in residence at Ulster University, carrying out a PhD examining revolution in high fantasy and tormenting everyone with yet more Pratchett quotes. If found, please give him a cup of tea and send him home via the nearest post office.

Follow Sam across social media as @pootsidoodle

GOG FROM MAGOG

Matthew A. Timmins

One spring day, Magog the giant was walking through the forest. He was gathering flowering tree branches into a bouquet for the supper table when he heard the most beautiful singing. He could not understand the words, but the music held him rooted to the spot, his huge hands dangling at his sides. He didn't dare to move lest he somehow disturb the music.

Slowly the music faded and Magog sprang to life. He ran through the forest, chasing the dying echoes, until he came to the base of a rocky cliff. In the cliff was a cave, and from this cave the singing could be heard growing fainter and fainter.

Without a thought for his best waistcoat, Magog crouched down and began crawling through the cave. It was a long, dark crawl but at last he saw daylight before him. He emerged in a forest the like of which he had never seen. The trees were tall—almost to Magog's chin—with white bark and leaves of silver and gold. Of the day's clouds there was no trace and the sunlit air sparkled like water. He could hear the singing clearly now, and he moved toward it, bending low beneath the treetops and tip-toeing, for he felt that he did not belong here.

He came to a glade were a sward of brilliant grass ran down to a pool of glistening water. Bathing within this pond was a giantess. It had been nearly 100 years since Magog had seen a giantess, and that had just been an aunt, but here was one now. And not just a giantess, but a beautiful giantess of statuesque proportions and snow-white skin. She was washing her flame-red hair and singing all the while with the voice of a siren.

Magog was entranced. He hid among the trees and watched and listened with rapture.

Suddenly the giantess stopped singing and looked straight at him with her big sapphire blue eyes. "Who spies upon my bathing?" she demanded.

Magog was gripped by panic. He tried to slip away but tripped over a boulder and fell backward with a crash.

"Come out, spy," she demanded. "Show yourself."

Scrambling to his feet, Magog stumbled out of the trees and stood before her. His heart rattled in his chest and his blood pounded in his ears, so that he could scarcely hear her.

"Well, spy." She stood waist deep in the water. "What have you to say?"

Magog opened his mouth but found his tongue thick and uncooperative. Flush and hot and unable to breathe, he threw his bouquet of branches at her and ran back the way he had come. He did not look behind him and heard nothing but his own heart. He came to the cave and threw himself upon the ground and crawled through the opening quick as a rabbit.

Back in the familiar forest, it was raining. Magog did not pause but ran all the way back to the cozy cottage where he lived with his brother, Gog.

When he slammed the door behind him, Gog looked up from the pot he was tending. "Why, brother, where have you been? The stew is ready and the table is all set."

"B-bathing," Magog stammered.

"You've been bathing? You don't look it," Gog surveyed his brother's torn waistcoat and dirty trouser. "And where are the flowers for the table?"

But Magog only shook his head and would say nothing till Gog had sat him down and fetched him a cup of tea. Then Magog told Gog all he had seen and heard.

Gog was silent for a long moment, then he rubbed his bald head. He was as hairless as an egg owing to unfortunate dealings with an dwarf.

"A giantess, you say? Well, well, this is interesting."

"Interesting?" Magog grew angry. "She was the most beautiful thing I've ever seen! And her singing could lull a dragon to sleep."

"Ho-ho," laughed Gog, "are you in love, brother?" He poked him in the ribs.

"And if I am?" Magog slapped his hand away. "I'm allowed to love a beautiful giantess, aren't I?"

"Is this why we have no flowers for our table? Did you present them to your lovely giantess?"

Magog hung his head in shame. "I didn't give her the flowers, I threw them at her."

"You *threw* them? Oh, Magog."

"Gog, I'm so embarrassed! When she caught me spying on her, I was as helpless as a rabbit. I couldn't talk. I could scarcely breathe. I just threw the flowers and ran away!"

"Never mind," said Gog. "Come and have some supper and you'll feel better."

But he didn't feel better. All during supper Magog could think of nothing but the beautiful giantess. Lying in bed that night, he imagined he heard her singing on the wind. The next day and all the following week he said little and ate less. He was, in fact, pining away.

Gog did what he could to distract his brother. He set Magog to gardening and fishing and helping in the kitchen. They played cards in the evenings and Gog sang bawdy songs. But it was no use: Magog was lovesick for want of the beautiful giantess.

"Well," said Gog one evening, "if you won't stop mooning over her there is only one thing to do: you must win her."

Magog looked horrified. "I couldn't, I mean, I can't. I couldn't face her again, not after I was such a fool!"

"It's the only thing to be done," Gog repeated. "You must have courage. Tell her your heart and perhaps she will feel as you do. After all, giants aren't so common that a giantess can afford to be choosy."

"I can't!"

"You can. But are you sure you want to?"

"What do you mean?"

"I mean, the last giantess we knew caused no end of bother."

"That was our aunt. Aunts are different."

Gog shrugged. "Then you must speak to her. Sing her a song, write her a poem, or *give* her some flowers."

A strange look came to Magog's eye. "Perhaps," he said slowly, "you could go for me."

"What?"

"You could be my em…em…something. Delivers messages and such."

"Emissary?"

"That's it! You could be my emissary! You could declare my love and present her with some token. Please say you'll do it!"

"I don't know," said Gog.

"Please, brother!"

Gog sighed and shook his head. "Very well."

"Oh, thank you! Thank you!"

"But you must write a letter and send a suitable gift. I'm no herald to be making pretty speeches."

~ * ~

It took Magog many days to gather the best flowers for a garland for the giantess's head and many more to write a letter for her heart but when he was done he presented them proudly to Gog.

"Very nice," said Gog, carefully slipping the garland into his satchel. Then he took the love letter and put it in his breast pocket.

Magog had told him where to go—northwest past the dead oak, west at the split boulder, through the cave at the cliff base. So, gripping his walking stick, a pine tree stripped of its branches and polished till it shone, and feeling just a bit foolish, Gog set out to find the beautiful giantess.

All day he walked, from red-skied morning to pale twilight, till he came to the cave in the cliff base, just as his brother had described. With a sigh, he got down on his hands and knees and began crawling.

At the end of the cave Gog came to the sunlit forest of sliver and gold, just as Magog had said. He marveled at the white trees and at the renewed day and knew, with a queer feeling in his stomach, that he was in a magical place. Fearfully, he went on.

Soon he came to the glade and the mere and the bathing giantess. She was everything Magog had said she was and more and for a moment Gog wished he had come wooing on his own behave. But the moment passed and Gog the Faithful stepped out from the trees and announced himself.

"Greetings and salutations, my good lady. I am the giant Gog from Magog, my brother."

"Stars and Stones!" exclaimed the giantess, "Another spy."

"I am no spy, my lady. I am an envoy from my brother, a giant of respectable character who er, approached you some days ago."

"Yes, I remember your brother." She stepped from the water. "Has he more pretty words to utter or gifts to throw at my feet?"

Gog blushed till his head looked like a huge radish. "Indeed, he has sent you this letter and this garland with hopes you will forgive his earlier behavior." Gog held out his brother's offerings.

She smiled dismissively at them. "And why should I care for

gifts from a *giant?*"

"Why?" Gog frowned, sending wrinkles scaling up his bald head. "Because you are a giantess, and he a giant. Naturally, when he saw you—"

"A giantess!"

"Er, yes?"

"I am no giantess, you want-wit!" Her eyes flashed. "The very notion!"

"You're not?"

"I am a subject of the Court of Grass and handmaiden to the Lady of the Red Ring." And with a flash of light and a smell of rain the giantess became a winged maiden no bigger than Gog's thumb.

Gog jumped backwards. "Stones preserve us! A fairy!"

~ * ~

While his brother was away, Magog fretted and paced. He had cleaned the cottage twice already. He had washed and combed his hair and his beard and put on his second-best waistcoat, since his best was still torn and stained with mud. Now he wrung his hands and looked from the clock to the door.

"She won't come," he said to himself. "Oh, but if she does!" He opened the door and looked into the starry night. "Where is Gog?" He closed the door hurried to the mirror. "She won't come," he said as he combed his beard again.

The door opened and he spun around, his face full of hope. But his hope deflated when he saw only Gog slumped against the door and breathing hard.

"Gog! What did she say? Did you find her? Where is she?"

"Oh, Magog," Gog panted.

"What is it? What happened?"

"Oh, Magog!"

"What is it? Did you give her my letter?"

"Oh, Magog!"

Magog grabbed his brother by the shoulders and shook him. "Speak, you parrot! What happened?"

"Let's sit, first," said Gog.

Magog hurriedly sat in a chair by the hearth and motioned for Gog to do likewise. "Now," he said. "Tell me what happened. Please."

Gog sat. "I followed your instructions and came to the silver and gold wood. There was the glade, and the lake, and…her."

"And?"

"We spoke and… Oh, Magog!"

"Don't start that again! Did you give her my letter? And the garland?"

"I tried, but she would not accept them."

"Why not?"

Gog took a deep breath, "because she is not a giantess, but a fairy."

"A fairy!" Magog bolted upright in his chair.

"Yes, brother, a fairy who can alter her size."

The brothers sat in silence for some moments.

"That explains her great beauty," said Magog.

"Indeed," agreed Gog. "The Fair Folk are as beautiful as they are dangerous."

"And her enchanting song," whispered Magog.

"Enchantment," nodded Gog gravely.

They fell silent again. Gog began to stoke the fire against the chill while his brother sat lost in thought, a strange sparkle in his eye.

"A fairy," he said softly. "Well, well," he smiled a sly smile. "And why not? It has been done before."

Gog turned around, a bundle of tree trunks in his arms. "Magog," he said warningly.

But his brother was lost in speculation. "And if she can alter her size… "

"Brother, no." said Gog sternly. "It is folly."

"Why? The Fair Folk have married men before. And if men, why not giants?"

"You're mad."

But Magog was not listening. "I shall write her a new letter, a better letter. And I shall make her a better present than a garland of twigs! Yes! And you will go to her again and…"

But Gog was not there. He had thrown down his firewood and gone out into the garden for a smoke.

~ * ~

For the next week, the brothers hardly talked. Magog spent all his days crafting a coronet of oak for his beloved's head and his nights composing a love letter fit for a fairy. Gog had spent Monday and Tuesday trying to reason with his brother but had given in by Wednesday and spent the rest of the week sulking.

Finally, on Saturday, Magog announced that he was finished. "There," he said proudly, holding up the wooden crown.

"Magog," said his brother in spite of himself, "it's lovely!"

And so it was, with delicate carvings of strawberry leaves and daisies, smooth marbled wood, and at its front a giant pearl which Magog had fished up from the sea floor.

"You must take this coronet and this letter to the fairy giantess with my never-ending love."

Gog looked at the beautiful crown and at the hope in his brother's face and relented with a sigh. "Very well, I shall go tomorrow."

~ * ~

Sunday dawned clear and bright, the world washed clean by yesterday's rain. Gog set out early, with his walking stick, a packed lunch, and Magog's crown and letter carefully tucked away in his satchel. He walked all day, saying to himself, "maybe the silver and gold wood will not be there." For he knew that magical places did not always stay where you left them. But alas, when he came to his journey's end he found the cave in the cliff face and at the end of the cave the white wood of silver and gold.

"Maybe," he said as he walked slowly through the wood, "the fairy is not bathing today." But alack, this hope proved as false as his last, for when he came upon the glade, there was the giantess-who-was-no-giantess bathing herself in the clear waters.

Gog had little experience with giantesses and even less with fairies. He stepped out of the trees and bowed stiffly. "My fair lady."

"Behold," she said, glancing back at him over her shoulder. "It is the spy's brother. Pray tell me, am I to forever more be plagued by giants?"

"My fair lady," he bowed again. "I have come again from my brother who sends tokens of love."

"Love?" She turned back to her washing. "Am I to be wooed by your dumb brother, then?"

"He has sent me as emissary to woo in his stead."

When he said this there was a sound like the tinkling of a dozen little bells and from around the lake, where they had been reclining in flowers and under leaves, sprang a dozen laughing fairies. They flew around the giant's head, tiny stars of purple and green and red.

"A giant, wooing," they cried in delight. "An ogre come a-courting!"

"Go away!" Gog frowned. "Leave be." He swatted at the fairies.

But they were too fast for him and only laughed the more. They began to sing a taunting song:

> *A giant come a-wooing*
> *A-courting and a-cooing!*
> *Hi-hiddle-he!*
> *What queerer sight to see*
> *Than a giant come a-wooing?*
>
> *A fish up a tree!*
> *A mouse with a saddle!*
> *An ogre come to tea!*
> *A parliament of cattle!*

They teased him with many more songs and mocked him and pinched him and needled him with their swords till he was nearly in a rage. He bellowed and swatted at them, his face red.

The giantess-who-was-no-giantess laughed along with the rest. But at last she held up her hands.

"Sisters," she said. "Sisters, enough. Let us hear what this giant has to say." She stepped from the water and donned a gown of white before approaching him. "Very well, giant, Gog from Magog, woo me."

As the fairies withdrew, Gog swallowed his rage. He was still bright red as he fumbled with his satchel. "Magog has sent you this crown and this letter." He held them out to her.

The fairy folded her giant arms. "Your brother has chosen his emissary well, for you woo nearly as well as he. Tell me, why should I marry your brother?"

"And why should he marry a wicked thing like you?" Gog said to himself.

But to her he said, "Magog is a noble giant, with a kind heart. There is skill in his hands," Gog said nodding at the coronet. "He is proud of bearing and," he searched for more, "he owns his own cottage by the sea."

"Proud of bearing," she laughed. "I hope he has more hair than his brother. I will not have a husband so bald as thee."

Gog laid a hand on his cheek. "No, my lady, Magog has a fine head of hair and a handsome beard."

"Very well, giant," she said, smiling to the fairies that flew about her. "I shall set you a challenge. Meet it, and I shall accept your brother's tokens of love. What's more, I shall send him one of my own."

"A challenge," The fairies cried excitedly. "A challenge!"

"A challenge?" said Gog, silently cursing his brother.

"Indeed," she smiled. "There is an apple tree that bears apples of silver and gold. Return to this lake with a silver apple from that tree before the sun rises tomorrow, and I shall be your brother's bride."

"And how do I find this tree, my lady?"

The fairy pointed to a tiny rivulet that emptied into the lake. "This stream springs from the roots of the tree."

Gog let out his breath. He had been much alarmed by the idea of a challenge, but now he almost smiled. To fetch an apple seemed no task at all for a giant! So he put the crown and the letter back in his satchel, bowed again to the fairy, and strode away, keeping the little stream between his giant feet.

He had not gone far before the wood of silver and gold came to an end and he found himself in a meadow of wildflowers. The air was sweet, the wind warm, the sky bright, and the stream clear and straight.

"Fiddle-de-fiddle-dum," Gog hummed. "Magog will soon have himself a fairy bride!"

He walked briskly. Soon he noticed the flowers of the meadow grew larger, daisies as big as his hand and poppies as tall as his knees. The stream too grew to a wide river and he was forced to walk along one bank instead of two. The further he walked, the larger the wildflowers and grasses grew. They were at his waist, and then his shoulders' and then they grew so great that they towered over the giant's head!

Gog stood bewildered. All his long, long life he had been the biggest of the big, except for a few dragons. Now the horizon was lost to view, the tiny stream had become a wild river, and lilies of the valley soared above his head like church bells!

"What has that cursed fairy done to me?" He said to himself. "Has she robbed me of my size, or sent me into a land gianter than giant?" Then, deciding that it hardly mattered which it was, Gog took up his walking stick and marched on.

It was a new and fearful experience, this mouse-sized view of the world, but Gog was angry now, and determined to meet the fairy's challenges.

"It will serve her right," he grumbled unkindly, "being married to a feather-head like Magog!"

~ * ~

While Gog was struggling across pebbles and under toadstools, Magog was rearranging furniture. He had moved Gog's bed into the spare room and was now positioning his bed— *"My future marriage bed,"* he thought with a blush—in the center of the room.

"But, oh dear," he said. "What if Gog does not like sleeping in the spare room?"

He was finding that there were many little difficulties about bringing home a wife. There had always been just himself and his brother. They were not used to guests and had but two of everything: two bowls for their stew, two mugs for their ale, two stools at their table, two chairs by the hearth. Now he needed to find a third of everything.

And what about size? Would his new wife be content in her giant size, or would she sometimes like to be fairy-sized? Would he have to carve her a tiny chair and a miniature bowl?

Would she bring things of her own? And where would they keep them? Their cottage may have been as big as a castle, but for three giants it would be awfully snug. Or, perhaps she would not want to live at the cottage at all.

That was a hard thought. He had lived in the cottage with his brother for many, many years. The notion of leaving them both behind made his eyes moist.

~ * ~

Meanwhile, Gog was hurrying upriver. The shadows were growing long around him and soon the sun would set. It was a difficult journey. Gog could not believe the number of obstacles the world held for the tiny creatures: the trickle of water was now a rushing river, nettle bushes formed impenetrable hedges, and field mice were the size of bears. Onward he struggled, flitting between boulder-sized pebbles and sheltering grasses, ever watchful for crows, weasels, or other such beasts. The ground rose as the sun set and soon Gog was following the river uphill by starlight. Around him, the night was alive with a hundred sounds—hoots, cries, and howls —each made unfamiliar and menacing by his diminished stature.

A new fear came over Gog then, the dread of little creatures for swift and silent death from above. With many a fearful look at the starry sky, he ran for the cover of a wild rosebush. He was sheltering within its thorny tendrils, searching the sky for the shadow of wings, when he heard a sound behind him. Turning around he saw a pair of glowing eyes studying him. Just in time, he dove to one side as the eyes lunged at him and an unseen mouth snapped at where he had been. Lying on his side, Gog heard the creature pass. And pass. And pass.

"A snake," thought Gog. "A snake is as good—or as bad—as a dragon to a mouse-sized giant!"

Frantically, he scrambled to his feet. He could still hear the snake moving through the rosebush, but the sound seemed to come from every direction at once. "No use running," he thought. "I can't see where I'm going and I have no idea where the beast is. Then I stand and fight." He broke off a thorn and held it before him like a sword.

"Hi! Serpent," he shouted. "Here I stand! Come and catch me if you can!"

Louder and louder came the noise of the snake, but still it came from all around him. He turned in circles trying to find it.

Suddenly the eyes were before him! With all his strength, Gog lunged at the eyes, his thorn before him. The eyes lunged, too, and Gog knew nothing but a weight that drove him back and down. He could see nothing and hear nothing but his own ragged breath. He was flat on his back with his thorn held straight above him. A great weight pressed down on him and his mighty arms trembled. With tremendous effort, he threw the thorn in one direction and rolled in the opposite.

He lay on the ground for some moments before he recovered enough strength to sit up. He was deep in the rosebush now and only the palest light filtered down from the stars. Reaching out and up with one hand he could feel the cold scales of his foe. But the snake did not move. He had slain it.

~ * ~

While Gog was battling the serpent, Magog was sitting by the fire reading a book he had found while cleaning the house. A frown wrinkled his face. The book was called *Tales of Fairy*.

"Oh, dear," he said after the first story.

"Oh, my," he said after the second.

"Oh my scented sandals," he said after the third story, putting the book down and staring long into the fire.

~ * ~

Gog was exhausted after the battle, but he dared not rest. The night was passing. So, plucking another thorn from the bush around him, he resumed his climb. He moved as quickly as he dared but he was weary now of wings and eyes and the rustle of grass.

Hours passed, and a moon rose into the sky, its light turning the river beside him silver. Then he saw it: a lone apple tree, seemingly growing from the river. The tree was still some way off but Gog ran toward it, abandoning caution.

He came to the top of the hill and the bottom of the apple tree and here, for the first time, he began to really despair. He could see the silver apples and the golden apples, but even the lowest were far above him. He sat down and tried to think. Nothing came to him but the taunting of the fairies and Magog's downcast face. Absentmindedly, he picked up a handful of pebbles and threw them one-by-one at the tree. He continued in this fashion till one of the tiny stones bounced off the tree and hit him on the forehead.

"Ow," he said, more surprised than hurt.

But the blow had given him an idea. Gathering up as many large stones as he could, Gog hunted out the lowest hanging silver apple. When he had found it he began throwing stones at the branch just above it. Though he hadn't done so in years, Gog used to be quite good at boulder tossing and though the boulders were now pebbles the principle was just the same.

Tock. Tock. Tock. Stone after stone struck true and before he had exhausted his stones the apple's stem broke and it fell to the ground. Gog rushed over to it. It gleamed like silver, as tall as the giant and twice as heavy. There was no way he could lift it, so he began to roll it back the way he had come. But the ground was rough and apples do not roll easily. Then another idea came to Gog and he rolled the apple towards the stream. With a mighty heave, he pushed the apple into the stream and jumped in after it.

The water was cold and fast. Gog struggled to catch the apple as it floated downstream, but catch it he did. He grabbed onto the stem and held on tight. The water rushed around, under, and over him, filling his ears and eyes so he did not know up from down or right from left. He was battered, bruised, chilled, and nearly drowned, but he did not let go of the silver apple.

After what seemed many waterlogged hours, Gog found himself washed ashore. He did not know where he was. He sat up and shook his head, wiping water from his eyes and knocking water from his ears. The raging river was nowhere to be seen. Neither was the apple.

"Where is it?" he cried.

Already, dawn was in the sky. Sunrise could not be far off. Frantically Gog scrambled to his feet and looked about him. Then he saw the tiny stream flowing between his legs and the grass under his feet. The world was its proper size once more. And clutched in his hand was a tiny silver apple.

"Hi-ho!" he cried. He glanced at the pink horizon, "and still time."

Then Gog ran down the tiny stream with great long strides. Even for a giant it was a long way to the mere where the fairies waited. But Gog was determined to meet the fairy's challenge. On and on he ran as the sky grew lighter and lighter. Soon he could see the lake and the sparkle of fairies like purple and red fireflies that hovered about it.

He could not discern Magog's fairy, and so—recalling the challenge—Gog leapt with all his strength into the lake, sending a deluge up into the air and raining down just as the sun peeked over the orange horizon.

"I have returned to the lake a silver apple!"

The fairies were not best pleased at their drenching and there was much muttering and talk of punishing the oaf, but Magog's fairy flew to Gog, standing in the middle of the lake. She was hardly bigger than the apple, but she took it lightly from the giant.

"Well met, giant," the fairy twisted the apple open. "You have met my challenge and I shall keep my word." She plucked a single seed from the apple. It sparkled like a gemstone. "Give this token to your brother and tell him to bring it back to me, here, in seven days' time, and I shall be his bride."

Gog took the apple seed. He thanked the fairy and went back through the white wood and through the dark cave and so back to the familiar world. He walked slowly and could hardly believe all that had happened to him. He kept taking the seed from his pocket and staring at it, shaking his head, and putting it away again.

"So Magog is to marry a fairy," he said to himself. "I suppose I shall have to move out of the cottage now. Or perhaps she will take him back with her to live in fairy-land."

He thought of Magog, alone in fairy-land, being teased and sung at.

"I suppose I won't see much of him from now on." He took the seed out of his pocket again. "I could throw this wretched thing away and be done with it. I could tell Magog I couldn't find her."

But, in the end, he put the seed back in his pocket and continued his journey.

When Gog got home it was late in the evening. Opening the door he found Magog seated by the hearth enjoying a pipe.

"Hullo, brother," he said.

Magog was overjoyed to see his brother alive and well. "Gog!" he shouted, jumping out of his chair and hugging his brother tight. "I missed you so, brother! Are you well?"

"Yes," said Gog. "I am well. What's more, I found your beloved."

"Ah," said Magog, looking uncomfortable.

"I gave her your token and she gave me one in return." He took the sparkling apple seed from his pocket and held it out to Magog. "She said that if you return with this seed in a week's time then she will be your bride."

"Oh," said Magog, shuffling his feet and fidgeting with his pipe.

"What's wrong?" said Gog. "This is what you wanted."

"The truth is," said Magog, "I've been thinking about marriage and about how one of us would have to leave the cottage... And I've learned a bit more about fairies. Oh, Gog, you've been so kind and you've gone through so much trouble and you're going to be awfully cross, but the truth is, the truth is, *I don't want to get married!* I want to live here, in our little cottage, with you, like always!"

Gog grew warm thinking of the trouble he gone through—the teasing and the snake and the drowning river—and then he looked at his homely cottage, the cheery fire crackling in the fireplace, and the pleading look on his brother's face.

"Quite right," he smiled at Magog. "Marriage isn't for the likes of us, and certainly not to a wicked fairy, no matter what her size!"

Gog flicked the apple seed into the fireplace, where it lodged between two stones. And sometimes, when it was raining, the seed would twinkle purple and green. Then Magog would watch it sparkle and dream of fairy-land and his lovely giantess until he shook the dreams away and got up to fetch another cup of tea.

~ * ~ * ~

Matthew A.J. Timmins lives in the wilds of Massachusetts with his lovely wife, who is only slightly wicked. When not writing, Matthew likes to wander about, keeping a wary eye out for fairies. His debut novel, *The Miseries of Mr. Sparrows*, was published in 2015 and his short stories have appeared in *Betwixt*, *Stupefying Stories* and *Unlikely Story* as well as multiple anthologies.

Matthew invites you to visit him at MAJTimmins.com and ~~stalk~~ follow him on Facebook.

che fiddler

H. A. Titus

The ocean was out there, sighing and swishing gently. I hadn't been this close to it since Da died.

I dumped my suitcase on the bed and crossed to the window. Pushed the frothy curtains aside and pressed my fingertips against the glass. Cold. My breath fogged on the glass, and I moved back so I could see.

The beach house sat on the top of a dune. Below me, ice-rimed grass bent toward the ocean. The hard, wet sand ran down the back of the dune and disappeared under a pile-up of ice. Beyond the ice, the ocean sighed.

Aaaah. Ssssh. Aaaah. Ssssh. A perfect four-four beat, Da had said. He'd loved the ocean in the winter. He'd stand out on the beach and sing, his deep voice ringing in time with the waves.

My little brothers thumped and thundered their way past my open bedroom door, shrill voices raised in a squabble about their video games.

Mom called for them to be quiet, but her tone was soft, lackluster. That meant she was probably doing the same thing I was, staring out at the ocean.

I stepped out into the small living room.

Mum stood at the French doors facing the ocean, her lined face soft. Tears quivered in the corners of her eyes, though a gentle smile curved her lips toward the crow's feet that were the sad echoes of her laughter.

Go ahead, Mum. I wanted to say. *You can cry.*

I'd yet to see her cry. I'd heard her, in the middle of the night when she thought everyone else was asleep and she could afford to be afraid. But I'd never seen her cry.

She turned and saw me, and the smile falsely widened. I liked her sad smile better.

"This is going to be a good vacation," she said, as if she was still trying to convince herself.

"Sure," I said.

Mum's lips quivered, and before she started crying she turned away. "Anthony? Davey?" she called. "Come help me unload the car."

The twins came out of their room in a tangle, eager to help Mum. I watched them head out to the car before turning back to stare out the French doors.

I turned back to the ocean. We hadn't been back here since Da had died. Two years without the ocean. A sudden desire to feel and smell it squeezed my heart. I unfastened the lock on the doors and slipped out, shutting it behind me, then ran for the beach.

I paused a few feet from the ice, which crashed onto the shore like some frozen white shipwreck. *Aaaah, ssssh, aaaah, ssssh* sighed the waves.

As I watched the ebb and flow, a high, ringing note pierced the air. I turned my head, my hair whipping into my face. The notes continued, a quick jigging tune that emanated from the cliffs to one side.

I jogged forward, straining to catch every bit of the song. It reminded me of the songs Da would play on cold nights when the wind howled around the house. Who could be playing the fiddle out here?

As I rounded the cliffs, I caught my breath in surprise.

It looked like winter hadn't even touched this area. The sand was clean, glistening golden from lanterns that floated in the air a few feet above my head. A long, low table sat, laden with steaming dishes, on a rug of seaweed. All sorts of people from Da's fairytales sat around the table—faeries, selkies, wood nymphs. At the end of the table sat a tall, young-looking man with a crown of seashells, and behind him stood the source of the music—a tall, broad-shouldered man with a five o'clock shadow. He held a bow in one hand, and with the other kept a fiddle tucked under his chin.

"Da?" I whispered, stepping from the frozen sand to soft, warm sand inside the summery circle. As soon as I did so, I felt a chill clamp around my soul. I was myself, and still not myself.

The fiddler changed, shrinking from Da's tall form to a stoop-shouldered, thin young man a few years older than me, his messy blond hair hanging in his gaunt face.

My heart stuttered. I tried to step back, but the sand shifted around my feet, holding me in place.

Before I could panic, the faerie king stood. "Welcome, mortal child. Would you care to join us?" He stretched his hand out toward me.

His voice was rich and smooth, like milk chocolate. I stumbled forward, my heart still hammering. To join them, to be allowed in their lovely company. Such a beautiful thought.

The fiddler shifted, catching my attention, and clarity burst over my head like a water balloon. My fingertips hovered over the king's for a split second, then I snatched my hand away. If I let him touch me, he would claim me. Da had always said the fae were tricky with their words, so I had to make sure my words were exactly what I meant to do. Then they couldn't trap me.

"I will join you for your *feast*," I said sharply.

The faerie chuckled. "A knowledgeable lass you are! We should be proud to have one so wise to our ways amongst us tonight, friends."

The rest of the table clapped and waved me over to an empty seat. As I walked across the sand to join them, the fiddler caught my eyes again. He stood biting his lower lip, his eyes glinting sadly out of the curtain of his hair.

The king turned to him. "Fiddler, another song!"

The fiddler reluctantly set his fiddle to his shoulder and his bow to his fiddle. He hesitated—the king frowned. The fiddler took a deep breath and began to play.

The fae placed a garland of flowers in my hair and gave me a cup of the most perfect juice I've ever tasted. They made sure my plate had the most delicacies on it.

At first, I was stiff and cold. The last thing I wanted was to lose my head and somehow be tricked into staying with the fae forever. Mum had suffered enough with Da's death—she didn't need me to disappear on top of it.

I shouldn't have worried. Every now and then, an off-key note —just slight enough that the fae never really took notice—would catch my ear over the chatter, and I would turn to look at the fiddler.

His deep, dark, sad brown eyes stared at me from his mop of hair. *Pay attention*, he seemed to be telling me. *Be careful.*

It always jolted me out of the hazy stupor I found myself falling into. And then his gorgeous music carried my mind away from the fae and the feast, and I would remember why I wanted to stay alert. Mum. The twins. There was no way I would leave them.

After a time that seemed both far too long and far too short, the faerie king stood up with his goblet in hand.

"Here's to my subjects for a merry feast. And here's to our mortal guest, Erika, who will provide us with entertainment for years to come."

My blood froze. "What?" I pushed my chair back from the table, stumbling. "How did you know my name?"

For the fae to know your name meant they had you completely in their power. I hadn't given him my name. He'd known it all along. I'd been under his enchantment all along.

Behind the king, the fiddler winced and stopped playing.

The king's lips curled in a thin smile. It tightened his face, making every bone stand out like a skeleton's, and gave a malicious glint to his eyes.

I balled my fists, turned, and ran. The sand turned hard and frozen under my feet, letting me dig in harder and run faster. I cleared the cliffs and dashed up the beach toward my family's house.

As I ran, I noticed the sky. It was turning green at the edge of the ocean. Sunrise was coming. I'd been out all night? What would Mum think?

I scrambled up the dune. The house stood further away from the dune than I remembered, with clusters of other houses and cottages on either side. That wasn't right. We didn't have a neighbor for a mile either way.

The door to the house eased open, and an old woman stepped out into the yard, carrying a tub of bread scraps. She dumped them in the yard, and from out of nowhere several gulls swooped down to pick at the scraps.

Mum hated seagulls.

I turned and stumbled down the cliff, tears blinding me. That wasn't Mum. This place had changed. And I knew it was the fae's fault. They'd done this for their *amusement*.

They were going to be sorry.

I made my way back to the cliffs, but their former feasting spot was empty. The sand was cold and hard. Ice piled on the waterline.

I flopped onto the sand, staring out into the ocean. Something cracked in my chest, as if my heart was breaking. Mum wouldn't know what had happened to me. She'd think I died, like Da. And I couldn't do anything about it. Tears dripped down my chin and soaked into the sleeves of my jacket.

Footfalls thumped on the sand behind me. I straightened and looked over my shoulder. The fiddler stopped a few feet away, his bow and fiddle dangling from one hand.

"I'm sorry, Erika," he said.

I should have been mad. He was the one who lured me there in the first place. But he'd also kept me as sane as he could. "You tried."

He sat down beside me and stared out over the icy, pink-and-orange-tinged waves.

"Will you get in trouble for talking to me?" I asked.

He shook his head. "It's the time between times. I'm free to do as I want." He shifted, and his deep eyes caught mine. "I'd like to help you."

"How?"

"There's a way to break the fae spell. No one else have been able to do it. But—" he cocked his head to the side and grinned. "For some reason, I think you might be able to. Do you want to try?"

"Why do you want to help me so much?"

"Because I'm not the fae. I don't like making people miserable." He rolled the neck of his fiddle in his hand and muttered, "Because I don't want people to share my misery."

"Is it dangerous?"

"Not particularly. Most people just can't do it. That's when it turns dangerous, because then the fae know that you can't escape, so they start tormenting you even more."

"I'll take that chance," I growled.

He rose and brought his fiddle up to his shoulder. "Okay. The fae love music, but they also hate certain types of it. What's the most powerful song you know?"

"How will that help?"

"Some things have power over fae," he said. "If done properly, it can break the enchantment. But I can't tell you what those things might be. You have to believe it in your own heart."

The most powerful song. I pulled my knees to my chest and bit my lip. What kind of power? There were songs that could make people cry or laugh—that was power over emotion. Songs Da used to sing that could shake the rafters of a church. The power of sound. What kind of power was he talking about?

Then I realized. A song that could make people smile or sob. A song powerful enough to vibrate glass yet could still be sung without waking a child. It probably wasn't nearly as powerful as the praises the *aingeals* sang, but I just knew—down in the core of my soul—that it would help me.

I lifted my face to the sky and began to sing. "Amazing Grace…"

The fiddler picked up the song, his instrument ringing out against the cliffs, strong and slow and vibrating down to my core.

As I sang, and he played, our song swirled around me. I clenched my hands in my lap and closed my eyes. I poured all my belief, all my heart, into that song, just like my Da had taught me.

As I sang and he played, the world around us shimmered. I saw two suns—one stayed stationary, just rising. The other sun flew through the sky, followed by the moon and stars. Days cycled past…

Months…

Years…

For a split second I thought I saw Da. A ghost image of him walking on the beach, his head thrown back in song. For a split second, my alto and his ringing bass combined.

When we've been there
Ten thousand years…

"Now, Erika! It's your time again—go!" the fiddler called.

I sprang to my feet and grabbed his hand. "You come too. We'll break out of the enchantment together."

He grinned and tucked his fiddle under his arm. We dashed together for the end of the bay. As the last note died off the cliffs, I slapped into a thick section of air.

It was hard to breathe. My feet slowed until I felt like I was in one of those horrible nightmares when a monster is chasing you but you're trying to run through something like molasses. I looked over my shoulder, and the fiddler was struggling even harder than I was.

Then I saw them. The fae stood just inside the bay, in the shelter of the cliffs, their eyes dark and hard. The fae king caught my gaze and grinned. His teeth had sharpened since the feast. He sunk his arm into the thick air and reached for the fiddler.

He saw the king coming and wrenched forward another step. It still wasn't far enough.

Amazing grace, remember! I thought.

I remember, he replied.

But he was tired and barely able to move. The king's hand was so close to him now, his eyes glittering. I swung around, reached out, and grabbed the fiddler's hand.

With a final prayer and a desperate heave, I staggered backward out of the thick air.

I could breathe again. I blinked, rubbed my eyes. The beach was grayed by the clouds overhead, and the waves still sighed through the ice piled at the edge of the shore.

"Am I back?" I whispered.

When I received no answer, I looked around. The fiddler had vanished. I spun back to the cliffs, but there was nothing there. The fae had vanished along with the fiddler.

My stomach knotted. Had he gotten away? Or had the faerie king managed to pull him back into enchantment?

A voice rang over my head. "Erika!"

I turned back around. Somehow, the thick, enchanted air had spit me back out closer to my family's beach house. Mum stood on the dune above me, holding a jacket tight around her body.

"Time to come in—you must be freezing!"

Mum was here! I was back in my own time! I ran up the dune and threw my arms around her.

"I love you, Mum."

"I love you too." I felt her wet cheek lean against my hair. Then she grasped my hand. "I have hot chocolate going on the stove. Let's go inside."

As I started down the dune, I heard a familiarly sweet, high note. I slipped my hand out of Mum's and looked over my shoulder.

Down at the water's edge, a young man in ragged jeans, bare feet, and a long-sleeved shirt held a fiddle tucked under his chin, his bow dancing across the strings. He spun on his heel and winked at me.

I grinned.

He finished his song and, with a flourish of his bow, waved.

"Erika, are you coming?" Mum called.

I waved back, then spun and tripped down the dune to the beach house. The smell of hot chocolate drifted out of the door Mum held open, I heard cartoons screaming on the TV inside.

Behind me, I heard the fiddle ring with the notes of *Amazing Grace*.

~ * ~ * ~

H. A. Titus can usually be found with her nose in a book or spinning story worlds in her head. She loves mythology, Dungeons & Dragons, and a good cup of tea. She lives in the Midwest with her weather-mage husband and two super-villain sons (don't mind the robotic dinosaurs, they're friendly) who enjoy dragging her on real-life adventures.

Some claim she is half-fae, but that's just unfounded rumor.

She draws from her knowledge of fairy tales and mythology from around the world to spin fantasy stories full of monsters, magic, and darkness that, somehow, still manages to show the bright light of hope.

Her newsletter, online blog, and serialized fiction and short stories can all be found at hatitus.substack.com.

pixie crystals

Irene Radford
writing as C. F. Bentley

In the annals of the Confederated Star Systems, the following events never happened and will not be acknowledged by any participants.

"Pixies. You think pixies have invaded the *First Contact Café*." Admiral Pamela Marella, spymaster for the Confederated Star Systems, buried her face into her palms, elbows propped on her desk. "You've had some crazy ideas in your life, Jake Devlin, especially since you took up with Sissy, High Priestess of Harmony, and found religion."

"Actually, the high priestess in question refuses to acknowledge this new alien life form as real." General Jake Devlin lounged against the door jamb of her secret office—the one no one, not even Jake, was supposed to know about. His responsibilities as commander of this space station might weigh heavily on his shoulders, but he still cut a roguishly dashing figure, tall and lanky with impressive abs and shoulders. He'd been Pamela's best spy, once. Then he met that pesky high priestess and became useless to her.

"So why are you telling me that pixies have invaded wing 25C?" She looked up, hoping he was simply playing a practical joke. The acolytes to the high priestess, who Jake treated as if they were his daughters, were notorious for such things.

"Because, dear Pammy, as spymaster it is your job to observe and record before first contact of a new alien species."

"Okay, I'll play along. Show me the recordings." Pamela leaned back in her chair and prepared for the worst.

Jake touched a button on his wrist link and aimed it at the screens on Pamela's desktop.

Suddenly the entire desk exploded in a mass of random pixels, then zoomed out until the individual bits of color resolved into a face. A cerulean blue face with hot, harem-pink hair. Pointed chin, ears, and up-tilted eyes stared back at her. The classic image of a pixie from her childhood storybooks.

She blinked and shook her head to clear it of one of her earliest memories. Long-ago memories, when magic was possible and reality of her own making. Now, she believed only what she could document. This recording appeared to be documentation.

"Maybe we should just give this place to the Dragons of D'Or, who think they hold a non-existent mortgage and therefore own the place. Let them handle all the mysticism and fairy tales that are taking over," she muttered, not caring if Jake heard her or not.

When she looked back, the blue face had moved away from examining the security monitors to flit back to the center of the room on impossibly flimsy, neon-green wings. It wore absolutely nothing, no clothes at all. Not even a loincloth to cover its—*his*—privates.

"Did he take fashion lessons from the Dragons of D'Or?" she asked, not knowing what else to say. They had only recently banished the banker dragons from the space station. Those large, obnoxious lizards took pride in parading around in the altogether, showing off battle/mating scars as points of honor.

"Yeah, I noticed the lack of clothing. Almost enough to make a mere mortal like me jealous. But that's not important. I'll zoom out again so you can see the entire area around the lift shaft." Jake touched another place on his link. The images shrank and the view expanded.

Six upright, pointed structures sprang into view, all placed in a circle around the lift.

"What are they made of?" Pamela leaned closer, tapping the icon to enlarge a specific area.

"Junk," Jake said.

"I can see that. Bits and pieces of construction material, and crystal shards, and even some leaves from the orange tree in the hydroponics garden. What are they doing?"

She half stood and craned her neck to see if an upside-down perspective made more sense. A thrill of shock rippled down her spine. "Jake, is this…is this…?"

"Yeah, they stole the black badger metal crystal stars right off my uniform collar. The most expensive things I own, and the first gift Sissy gave me."

"Not to mention that when badger metal is added to a crystal matrix, it augments communication waves exponentially through hyperspace. We can talk to each other almost instantaneously across light years." Pamela had lusted over those stars for years. Sissy had taken them right off her ceremonial beaded veil. With those stars, or even with a shard from them, she could do so much more in organizing her field operatives.

Then a new thought pierced her awestruck brain. "Jake, are they building communication towers?"

"Could be, could be." His face remained professionally blank, which meant she'd surprised him with the idea. "Want to go look in person?"

Jake aimed for the door, automatically checking the pockets within pockets within pockets of his everyday black uniform. He always had at least three perpetually sharp badger metal blades on him somewhere.

Pamela mimicked him, adding various projectile, energy, and thrown weapons to empty places in the "civilian" professionally casual jacket and trousers she'd made into her own uniform without being a uniform. That's what spymasters did.

Her wing looked abandoned on any space station sensor, but actually bustled with activity. She checked the sensors so they showed the lift stopped, its continually rotating platforms idle and gathering dust. Silently she and Jake traveled upward to the zero-G station hub, then across three tram stops to the 25C wing. A quick review of the station map showed this wing and the two adjacent ones, 25A and 25B, were empty but warming and filled with atmosphere. No airlock above the blast doors, so the incoming aliens breathed something non-toxic. The place was ready for the arrival of a diplomatic mission from…from…

"Am I reading this right, Jake?" she asked, slapping her forehead in dismay.

"Diplomatic mission consisting of three ambassadors, each with three mates and three assistants, from Ælbion. Please tell me that isn't pronounced 'elven.'"

"Have they arrived?"

"No. Their ship hasn't even broken hyperspace, and shouldn't until day after tomorrow."

"This is taking on all the symptoms of a cosmic joke," Pamela grumbled.

"Yeah, I know." Jake looked ecstatic rather than dismayed. "Isn't it great?"

Pamela stepped onto the next rotating platform headed down into the dark depths of the 25 wing. Jake followed, squeezing into the confined space of the lift beside her.

"Do you suppose these critters are ancient refugees from Earth?" he whispered.

"No." But those pictures in her story books...

"I've got one of the improved universal translators. I wonder if the memory will play back an ancient Earth language, like Anglo-Saxon or some such."

"You're getting too caught up in this, Jake. Think like the trained military tactician and pilot you are, not the mystic consort of a high priestess."

"Part of being Sissy's mystic consort is awakening a sense of wonder in life. All life, even alien life. Finding that joy again is important. You should try it sometime, Pammy."

Jake was the only person alive who got away with calling her 'Pammy.' Well, maybe Sissy and her acolytes. But no one else. No one!

Light leaked upward in the lift shaft.

"This wing is supposed to be dark," Jake whispered, reaching for a mini-blaster holstered on his belt above the right hip.

Pamela toyed with her own version in the patch pocket of her suit jacket.

Down through the first two levels of light gravity they rode the lift. The light grew ever brighter. Pamela's eyes adjusted as they descended. She broadened her stance, ready to leap or run the moment they reached LG4, the first level with gravity heavy enough that humans couldn't fly. The docking bay for this wing lay below LG5, as a transition to MG, or medium gravity.

Jake stepped off the platform and moved forward two steps, giving her room to follow. The lift continued its perpetual rotation down into the docking bay, before returning upward to the hub. To catch the upward lift, they would have to walk around to the other side of the mechanism, or take the spiral stairs that wound around the shaft.

Something buzzed Pamela's hair. She swatted at it as she would an errant mosquito if she were dirtside.

"Did you import insects for the hydroponics garden?" she

whispered to Jake.

He ducked another flying thing before replying. "Yes, and the pixies were in the garden if they found orange leaves. Probably didn't close the screens when they left."

Another buzz circled Pamela's head three times. She stood very, very still, as she'd been taught as a child at summer camp, to avoid bee stings.

The *thing* paused and hovered in front of her nose. Her eyes crossed trying to focus on it.

"Should have brought my reading glasses," she growled. Jake was the only one who knew she needed help reading, although not enough to take three days off work for corrective surgery.

The buzz took up a different cadence.

"Stay still, Pammy. I think it's talking." Jake held the palm-sized translation gadget level with the blurry, flapping pixie.

Loud squawking static blasted from the translation unit. Pamela flinched at the irritating noise. Jake dialed back the volume. Still static, no words.

"We are trying to understand you." He spoke slowly and distinctly into the device. "Please speak more words so that this machine can learn from you."

More static. It came out in an angry and emphatic tone. Pamela had a sudden urge to flee. Pressure built up in her chest, and her feet itched to run.

"Maybe we should go and come back with a telepath?" she suggested, inching backward and around the lift to the upward-moving platforms.

"Not without my stars," Jake said. He looked around frantically until his gaze caught the distinctive gleam of badger metal crystals in the tallest pile of junk behind and to his right. He backed toward it.

Inch by inch, he edged away from Pamela and the pixie. The alien ignored him. As long as he kept his movement slow and fluid, he seemed a natural part of the landscape. The broad open space should have been a neutral gray with portable partitions stacked on the deck awaiting assignment to separate the lobby of the lift area from rooms. The incoming aliens would arrange those partitions as they needed.

Then it hit Pamela. The pixies had painted the walls with tiny streaks of green. It reminded her of paintings she'd seen of open meadows with pin pricks of color that might be wildflowers.

Jake shifted the universal translator, which wasn't so universal after all, to his left hand and reached with his right. Ten pixies materialized in front of him, swooping in from all directions so rapidly that Pamela barely noticed their movement.

Jake, idiot that he was lately, kept moving his hand until he grasped one of two elusive black stars between two fingers. A scarlet and emerald and purple pixie dove for that hand.

MINE!

"Ouch! Oh, ow ow ow ow." He jerked his hand away and started sucking on the back, near the thumb joint. "The damned beast bit me."

The pressure in Pamela's chest increased along with the itch in her feet. An incredible sense of violation overwhelmed her.

"We have to leave now, Jake. We'll come back with a telepath," she said as calmly as she could. "An empath would be better."

~ * ~

Pamela paced Jake's office while he moved icons around on the desktop with his left hand. As a pilot, he'd had to become ambidextrous to manipulate the controls. His right hand was currently occupied by his wife. Short, wispy, and sometimes mousy, she did what she did best—take care of Jake. Within seconds of Jake sitting at his desk, she had appeared with disinfectant, anti-biotic patches, and bandages.

"What do you mean, there are no available telepaths? Last I looked, we had twenty-four registered onboard," Jake yelled at the database on his center screen.

"You sent them all back to Earth," Sissy reminded him. "Except for three who are still trying to decipher the Maril language."

"I'll take those. Similar situation, initiate communication with a totally alien race," Pamela replied.

"No. My daughter is part of that team. I will not expose her to those rabid pixies." Jake thumped the desk with a clenched fist. Icons bounced, rearranged themselves, and settled into a new order.

"Oh! Pammy, you've got to see this." He pointed to a screen showing the pixies in 25C.

Sissy leaned over Jake from behind, hand resting lightly on his shoulder. Disgusting. Any time they were together, they touched, as if reattaching their other half.

Pamela looked at the screen anyway. The pixies were there, all right. They seemed to have multiplied in the ten minutes since she and Jake had left them. And the junk towers! They'd added a cross-bar connecting two of them at the top. Another arced plank lay on the deck between two others. The top pieces seemed to have been woven together with bits of ripped, bright red sparkling cloth from… From her favorite formal diplomatic evening gown. The one that was lined with fine titanium mesh for added protection from projectiles or blades. It also had pockets secreted among the flowing drapery for weapons of her own.

"There's your other badger metal star, Jake." Pamela pointed to a bit of black glitter that scintillated differently from her red sequins.

"Look there, they are embedding the badger metal in the exact center of the lintel. The other one was in the center of an upright, 180° from it." Jake pulled up a calculator and began sliding numbers around in arcane patterns.

"I'll go get Martha," Sissy said. She must have recognized the deep concentration in Jake's posture and unblinking stare. Not much penetrated the man when he got that look.

"Pammy, get me the coordinates of 25C LG4."

"How precise?" She opened a new screen on his desk and began searching maps and tactical displays.

"To the millimeter of the center of that circle of junk towers," he murmured distractedly.

"I need my own computer."

"Don't care where you get the numbers, just send them to me within the next thirty seconds."

Pamela hunched over the screen and typed an encrypted command that linked her desk to this one. Easy. She did it all the time, usually from her desk so she could monitor what he was up to.

"I changed my encryption this morning. You won't find any-thing interesting with that string of numbers," he said as if asking for cream and two sugars in his coffee. He took it black.

She fed the system another string of numbers, and the tactical display she wanted popped into view.

"Wow, I can't get resolution that good, and I run this place." Jack whistled as he scanned her display. His right hand added the coordinates he wanted while admiring the rest of the view.

"You only think you run this place," Pamela replied. She watched as he triangulated the coordinates for the center of the pixie towers, then projected outward.

The computer churned and processed, throwing long strings of alphanumeric code onto the screen at random intervals. Pamela recognized some of them.

"Is the trajectory headed for Earth?" She frantically enlarged graphs and star maps on her own section of the desktop.

"Looks like," Jake said on a long exhale. "From this distance, I can't get any closer than the northern hemisphere."

"Maybe I can narrow it." Pamela called up her own, supposedly secret, com towers in Europe, North America, and Siberia. Then she layered satellite views and maps over their displays.

"Europe," she muttered. "Northwest Europe."

"England." Jake refined her data. A long pause.

"Is that Stonehenge?" Pamela pointed at the ancient monument, preserved inside a stasis field and off limits to all but the most privileged researchers. After thousands or years of research by archaeologists, spiritualists, and conspiracy theorists, its original purpose remained unknown.

"Yeah, the mother of all standing stone monuments," Jake replied. "And I've seen similar structures on a dozen different planets, but never in a space station."

The hatch to the outer office irised open to admit Sissy and fourteen-year-old Martha, the telepath Jake had adopted last year.

"You coming, Pammy? Or are you going to monitor this from the safety of your own office?" Jake asked as he moved to join the two newcomers.

"I'm coming. You couldn't keep me away." She had trouble reconciling the beneficent and friendly pixies in her story books with the angry, malevolent, thieving pests in 25C. Her favorite dress might be ruined, but she'd be damned if she left it with the monsters.

Jake rubbed at the bite wound on his hand as if he agreed with her. He still had some incredibly valuable and emotionally significant star-shaped badger metal crystals to retrieve.

They explained the situation to Martha while they traversed the station to the infested wing. She nodded and smiled until Jake came to the part about the bite.

"Let me see the holos," Martha said, slipping her arm through

Jake's. Their close relationship still amazed Pamela. One would almost think he was her biological father and not an adopted one. "Pammy?" she asked, using Jake's insolent nickname, "what did you feel when you tried to get close to the towers?"

"What does that matter?" Pamela stilled, unwilling to accept this invasion of her privacy.

"That scary?" Martha asked impudently.

Damn, her telepathic powers heightened and honed every time Pamela encountered the girl. A single telepath within the ranks of her spies would be *the* most useful tool and a powerful weapon. Power-lust invaded her so fiercely that she almost couldn't see where she set her feet. Dangerous as they approached the constantly moving platforms of the lift.

But this girl had ethics about invading other people's minds. Pamela's thoughts about the chest pressure and urge to flee had been very close to the surface. Martha would probe no deeper without permission or dire emergency.

Did this invasion of pixies classify as an emergency? Jake pressed his wound tightly, as if to contain the pain.

The lift descended into 25C more rapidly than Pamela wanted. Her mind told her the mechanism moved at the same speed as ever, but her guts wanted to linger, delay.

"Incoming!" Jake ducked and rolled off the lift.

A half second later, Pamela heard the buzz and felt the brush of feather-light wings against her cheek. In her peripheral vision, she caught an impression of bared teeth in the middle of a puke-green face.

Pressure built within her chest with twice the intensity as her last trip here. As she mimicked Jake in avoiding a fierce bite, she noted the holographic number displayed on the walls of the lift. LG3, a full level above the towers under construction.

"Sissy!" Jake screamed as his wife and daughter disappeared downward in the relentless rotation of the lift. He jumped to his feet and grabbed the railing of the spiral staircase in one fluid motion. Without a pause, he perched on that railing and let gravity propel him downward almost as quickly as the lift.

Pamela followed him. If she walked down the steps, she'd have time to give in to the compulsion to flee. She slid around the last curve before the spiral and the lift terminated at black doors, separating this portion from higher gravity, in time to watch Sissy and Martha step off the lift, pictures of feminine calm.

Jake leapt free and flung himself between his family and the towers, which appeared to have grown in the short time since she'd watched them from Jake's office. Her eyes went to the glint of badger metal crystals embedded in one tower to the red sequins woven through all six towers. Added to those features, she saw six of the helmet lights beloved by maintenance workers the galaxy wide. The pests liked their bling.

Martha stopped two steps away from the lift and held up both hands, palm out, level with her ears. The pixies held their positions, wings working to keep them in place. One by one, two dozen of them at least, dropped to the deck in a close circle around the telepathic girl.

Jake and Sissy froze in place. Pamela did, too, though the pressure on her lungs and the itch in her feet really wanted her to turn around and leave the other three to handle the situation.

"Dad, can you try the translator again? I'm getting lots of sharp syllables and very few images," Martha asked.

Slowly, Jake drew out the palm-sized device and thumbed up the volume. Static gave way to harsh, throat-gargling consonants.

"I understand some German," Pamela admitted. "That sounds close. But I can't find any one word there that I recognize."

A second later, the translator repeated her words in the same throat-ripping garble.

"That's progress, of sorts," Pamela said.

The pixies rose in a flurry of wings, weaving rapidly among themselves in a pattern too complex for Pamela to discern. Only there was a pattern.

"Martha, can you project a nice, peaceful image to calm them down?" Sissy whispered.

"Like what?" The girl sounded frustrated.

"Flowers. You like roses," Jake urged her.

Pamela had set up monitors near the circle of rose bushes in the hydroponics garden. Martha spent a lot of time there, 'meditating.' Whatever that meant.

The translator erupted with noise. Martha backed up, hiding her head beneath crossed arms.

"Roses, evil. Bad, bad, bad," she said, sounding more than a little panicky. Then she followed up with a series of explosive sneezes.

"I think the pixies are allergic to roses," Pamela said, finally finding the courage to step down from the last stair and onto the deck. Her left hand fingered a mini-blaster in her jacket pocket.

Sissy put her arms around the girl and pulled her face into her shoulder.

"Well, that didn't work," Jake agreed, moving to wrap both his wife and daughter in a protective hug.

"Wait," Martha said, looking up and around. "Who is supposed to move into this wing?"

"A new race we haven't met before, the Ælbion," Jake said.

Pamela tried to follow the agitated pixies's flight path. It looked… It looked like classic piloting evasive maneuvers, the kind taught at the Academy. Everyone knew those tactics, and predicted them with accuracy. Now, she taught her operatives to use their imaginations and not be so predictable. Jake had taught her the value of that strategy.

"A-ee-l-bee-n?" Martha tried the name phonetically. The pixies didn't vary their pattern at all.

"Martha, try El-ven," Pamela suggested.

She'd barely finished the last sound when the pixies exploded with a loud chatter that made her throat ache just thinking about replicating the words. Pixies began circling each tower in a giant spiral. Her ears popped with changing air pressure. The remaining cross-lintels levitated into place without anyone touching them. Something about the flight path and flapping wings must create an energy field.

Then the pressure in her chest doubled. She had to drop to her knees to keep breathing. Why weren't the others affected? Wait, Jake panted shallowly. Sissy and Martha, however, were so focused on understanding the pixies that, if they felt the chest pressure, they ignored it.

"Wh-what are they doing?" Pamela gasped.

"It's not like that at all!" Martha shouted as she stamped her foot and placed tightly clenched fists on her adolescently slim hips.

"What is like that?" Pamela ground out.

"You're just selfish bullies with no manners," Martha continued her tirade. Then she had to duck and cover, dragging Sissy down with her.

"We've got to get out of here, fast," Sissy said. "They don't like us at all." She dragged Martha toward the lift.

Martha turned back at the last second and shouted at the pixies in their own language. Pamela didn't need to know the words to recognize the insults. The pixies knew it, too, and blew raspberries at their retreating backs from the safety behind the towers.

They made it back to Jake's office in record time. He'd left the monitors recording. Pamela planted herself in his chair and flipped icons around to suit her own work routine. Jake spent his attention on comforting Sissy and Martha. He did it well. Fine. That left the desk and computing power to Pamela.

"Um, Jake, you need to see this." She had to rest her head against the back of the chair.

When she dared open her eyes, she found Jake hunched over the desk, propped on his elbows, hands flat against the reflective surface.

"That can't be! We have to figure out how they are doing this!" he said.

"Their message is beaming back to their planet of origin, and using the home beacon to bounce their signal back out into the galaxy to all of their colonies," Martha said. She sounded exhausted. Sissy guided her to one of the guest chairs. The gel pads shifted to conform to her body.

"What are you saying?" Pamela asked as she tracked the energy pulses emanating from wing 25C of the *First Contact Café*. The message moved with the speed of a badger metal-enhanced ansible. Nearly instantaneous across thousands of light years. If she had access to that kind of communications network, she could run the entire C. S. S. from her desk!

The searing white light paused when it reached the ancient monument known to humans as Stonehenge. Some of the original stones had fallen, others broken or repurposed into building material. Still the energy circled around and around, much as the pixies had circled their miniature replica. Ten circles—she counted without blinking, for they moved too fast to chance missing something.

"This is too much," Jake said. One of his fingers traced the images on the desktop. The solid beam of light and energy separated into a dozen strands and began weaving a complex pattern around the monument. "That's the same flight pattern we watched the pixies fly."

"You noticed," Pamela said, trying to mask her awe with dry humor.

"Yeah, I noticed. I wonder if the pixies learned it from the Academy or if our military learned it from the pixies?"

"Don't wonder, just watch," Pamela ordered.

"No safe haven," Martha murmured.

Pamela didn't dare look toward the girl. The strands of energy had woven their fabric of communication and separated once more, each shooting out into space in a different direction.

"Where's it going?" Jake asked.

"You said you'd seen similar monuments on a dozen different planets?"

Jake nodded, eyes crossed as he thought about the implications.

"Twelve strands of energy, each in a different direction. I'll bet if we plotted the trajectories, they'd end at those monuments."

"No safe haven," Martha repeated. "Humans infest space. Humans bring killer roses. Elves making peace with them. No safe haven. Get out now!"

The memory of cherished picture books from an innocent childhood crumbled in Pamela's mind.

~ * ~ * ~

Irene Radford has been writing stories ever since she figured out what a pencil was for. A member of an endangered species—a native Oregonian who lives in Oregon—she and her husband make their home in Welches, Oregon where deer, bears, coyotes, hawks, owls, and woodpeckers feed regularly on their back deck.

A museum trained historian, Irene has spent many hours prowling pioneer cemeteries deepening her connections to the past. Raised in a military family she grew up all over the US and learned early on that books are friends that don't get left behind with a move. Her interests and reading range from ancient history, to spiritual meditations, to space stations, and a whole lot in between.

Mostly Irene writes fantasy and historical fantasy including the best-selling *Dragon Nimbus* Series and the masterwork *Merlin's Descendants* series. In other lifetimes she writes urban fantasy as P.R. Frost or Phyllis Ames, space opera as C.F. Bentley, and steampunk as Julia Verne St. John.

If you wish information on the latest releases from Ms.

Radford, under any of her pen names, you can subscribe to her newsletter: www.ireneradford.net. Promises of no spam, merely occasional updates and news of personal appearances.

Che Cies Chac Bind

Sarah Joy Adams

In third grade, I came home from school on St. Patrick's Day and told my mom all about four-leafed clovers and the leprechauns who hid gold coins at the end of the rainbow and danced on the green with good little children. In dry L. A., where March meant the rains were already over, rainy Ireland already sounded magical enough. Why not believe in leprechauns, too?

"And who told you that load of crap?" she said, leaning against the kitchen counter with a highball glass in her hand. Her Irish accent was always stronger when she was angry.

"My teacher," I said, not so sure of it all now that I had said it out loud.

She laughed, one sharp *Ha!* Then she told me that leprechauns were sly little bastards who stole salmon from weirs and babies from cradles. They had no souls left to go to heaven with because God tossed them out after they wouldn't say yea or nay to Lucifer when he rebelled. Now all they had to treasure was the cold earth and their gold. "If you ever see one of them, you run the other way, you hear me?"

"Sharon!" Dad came into the kitchen and took the whiskey bottle back. "Don't tell her those things."

"Happy Anniversary to you, too," she said and saluted him with her glass and middle finger. She threw the highball glass in the sink and went outside to sit by the far side of the pool. She stayed there, staring at the tops of the palm trees while the sun went down. Dad got us kids our dinner and baths, and tucked us into bed.

He went outside. Their voices drifted through the bedroom window, too soft to hear properly, too harsh to ignore. She was crying. After a while he came back in and turned on the news.

My sister Caeli was already asleep. I tiptoed down the hall and slid the patio door open a crack. Mom sat on the pool steps, her feet in the water. The moonlight made silver and grey shadows across her body.

"Mommy," I whispered.

"What is it, puppy?" She liked to call us her pups when Dad wasn't around.

"I can't sleep."

She nodded and held out her arms. Cradling me like I was a baby, she slid into the pool. We floated, rocking back and forth like a boat on a calm ocean, and she sang the stars into the sky.

~ * ~

Whenever Dad went on a business trip, we kids would sit on the bed and watch him pack. We made a game of trying to distract him. "Don't forget your socks," we'd say, hiding the ones he'd already packed behind our backs.

"You already packed your razor."

"No he didn't!"

"I've got your toothpaste!"

"You can't take this tie, Daddy. This is my tie." My little sister wrapped Dad's ties around her head four or five at a time, until she looked like a Technicolor mummy.

"Okay, King Tut," Dad said. "Give me back the red one, at least." He snapped the garment bag in place and zipped up the suitcase. Mom stood leaning against the bedroom doorframe, a half-smile on her face. My brother Davy lay on the bed, kicking his feet against the pillow.

"You forgot your secret box, Daddy," he said. "You always take it."

Dad started. "Why, so I did," he said with a little laugh. He looked across the bed at my mother. "But maybe I don't need to take it with me this time."

She shrugged and walked away. Outside, the cab to take him to the airport honked. Dad grabbed the steel box, half the size of a shoebox, off the top shelf of his closet and stuffed it into his carry on. He kissed each one of us on the tops of our heads and said, "Don't swim too far out and watch for rip tides, okay?"

I pretended I didn't know what he meant, but Caeli and Davy agreed loudly. They followed him to the front door, dragging his suitcase between them.

At the door he kissed my mother good-bye, his fingers twined in her hair. "I love you," I heard him say.

"I love you, too," she said, but she wouldn't look up to meet his eyes.

He pulled her closer, nestling her face against his shoulder and for a second I hated her. Hated her like the sun burning out of the L. A. sky on a July day. He was a good Dad. He loved her. She ought to love him back. She owed it to him.

"Be careful with the kids," he said. "They can't swim like you can."

She kissed him on the cheek, a dutiful wife. "Don't miss your plane."

He slung his bag over his shoulder and trotted out to the cab. He waved to us all as it pulled away.

The minute he was gone, mom straightened. She took a deep, sharp breath like she scented something good over the horizon.

"Okay, kids. Last one in the car is a rotten egg!" And we ran, scrambling for bathing suits and sunscreen, sunglasses and water wings.

~ * ~

I was thirteen. The Lopezes came for dinner. Mom served salmon with boxty and colcannon.

"Now this is real Irish food," Dad said. "None of that corned beef stuff."

"That's not really Irish?" Mr. Lopez said.

"Sure it is. The way Taco Bell is Mexican," Mom said. All the grown-ups laughed.

Davy, Caeli, and the two Lopez boys were eating at the kids' table, which was the coffee table with pillows on the floor around it. Technically I was eating with them, but I refused to sit on the floor. Instead I slouched on the couch, feet on the floor, my back horizontal and my plate on my stomach, eyes fixed in a glare at my mother's back. They could banish me from the grown-up table, but they couldn't make me eat with these babies.

Joey Lopez made faces and poked at the colcannon. "Ew. Gross."

"It's potatoes and kale," I said. "It's good." *You rude little shit.*

He stuck out his tongue at me.

"Eat it. I dare you." His brother poked him, giggling.

"You eat it."

"No, you."

"No, you!"

"You infinity!"

They started pushing each other. Davy and Caeli pulled their plates away from the spreading squabble.

"So how did you two meet?" Mrs. Lopez said to my Dad.

"On a moonlit beach in Cork," Dad said. "I was doing a study abroad course in oceanography."

"Ooh, was it love at first sight?"

"It certainly was for me." He took my mother's hand, his thumb rubbing across her wedding ring.

She gave him a smile that might have fooled the Lopezes and took another drink of her whiskey. "There's one boxty left in the pan. Can I tempt anyone?"

"Oh, come on, Sharon. I want to hear the story. What were you doing out on a beach at night?" She elbowed mom and winked.

Mom, her hand still captive in Dad's, said, "I was taking a stupid risk."

Davy, Caeli, and I sat up straighter. I kicked the nearest Lopez in the ribs. "Shut it, you two."

"Ooh. Skinny dipping?"

Mom raised her drink again. "In a manner of speaking."

"Now, Sharon…" Dad said. She shrugged, that elaborate fluid shrug only she could do.

"It was Midsummer. I was young and curious. So I ignored my mother's advice and went out walking where I shouldn't have been. And that's when I met himself. He lent me his coat and bought me a drink in a real pub. I'd never been in a car before or seen a telephone. We spent a whole week together." She paused and looked at Dad, one hand still in his, the other stirring the ice in her glass.

We were all frozen, waiting. But Dad especially had eyes only for her. *Please*, they seemed to say. *Please don't.* I didn't know why her story made him afraid, why his hand was trembling, but I wanted to hurl my plate at her. *Say you fell in love. Say it!*

"After that," she said, "I couldn't leave."

Mrs. Lopez sighed and smiled, pressing her hands over her heart. Mr. Lopez laughed and punched Dad in the shoulder with a wink. Dad laughed back, but half his mouth refused to smile. The littler Lopez boy punched his brother and they fell on each other, knocking Kool-Aid onto Caeli's dress. Caeli shrieked. Mom knocked her chair over, she jumped up so fast. It was no problem, no problem at all, a little soda water and everything would be fine. Everything would be alright.

~ * ~

Mom taught me to drive on the PCH. We roared up and down the coast between Malibu and Santa Monica in the cream and blue convertible Dad had bought her for their last anniversary, me grinding the gears and Mom leaning back against the passenger seat like a movie star. Her black hair had always been gray-flecked, but she refused to color it. At Dad's insistence, she wore her nails red, though. Without the polish her nails were black, hard, narrow and elegant. Mine were like Dad's, flat and transparent, brittle.

"Let's get ice cream," she said.

"I'll get fat. I'm already fat."

She made a noise in the back of her throat. "What's wrong with a bit of fat?"

"Mom!"

We were driving past a stretch of rocky coast, full of tidal pools. She nudged me. "Pull in here. Let's go for a walk."

"I'll ruin my shoes."

"So go barefoot." She pulled off her own shoes and skipped down the rocks, broomstick skirt swirling. A group of fishermen turned to stare at her. One of them whistled.

Grouching and rolling my eyes, I scrambled after her. By the time I'd caught up to her she'd found a perch on a black rock warmed by the sun and sprayed by the ocean.

"Mom, we're getting wet."

"Mmmmm." Her eyes were closed, basking.

I gave up and sat beside her, leaning against her arm. Something silver and black bobbed up in the surf and disappeared. It re-appeared closer, big dark eyes above the waterline, and was gone in a flash of tail flippers.

"Puppy, when you grow up…" She paused and frowned at the waves. "Are there any boys you like?"

I wriggled beside her. *Yes. But if I tell you about him he won't be my secret crush any more. You'll invite him to dinner and Dad will make dumb jokes and Caeli and Davy will ask him questions like do you like kissing?"*

"Maybe," I said. The seal popped up again, closer. Short whiskers flicked above the water. A snort and it was gone again. Another, beige and black, popped up closer.

"Don't marry him."

"Mom! I'm still in high school." Pages of my secret, locked diary were covered in *Mrs. Roger Bell. Mr. and Mrs. R. Bell. Mrs. Bridgid Bell. Captain and Mrs. Roger Bell.* My classmate Dolores was already engaged. They were going to get married as soon as he came back from Vietnam.

She sat up suddenly, grabbing my hand. "I'm serious, Puppy. Sleep with him if you want to. It's okay. I'll get you the pill. Your dad doesn't have to know."

"But we're Catholic."

"So go to confession, if it makes you feel better. But don't let him keep you. Don't let him get a part of yourself that he can hold onto forever. Do you understand me?"

I jerked my hand away from hers and scrambled to my feet. "Some people actually love their husbands! What if I want to get married and have lots of babies and be happy instead of drinking whiskey and moping around all day? What about that?"

Her normally pale skin was grey. "I tried to be happy. I did try…"

"No you didn't. All you ever do is make snarky jokes and say things with double meanings. Dad gives you everything! You should be grateful a man like that loves you."

"I gave him three children. That was the bargain!"

"Then why don't you leave?"

"Because I can't! Don't you understand?"

"No!"

She held out her hands like she would hug me, but I shoved her away. Her bare feet slipped on the rocks. She flailed, arms pinwheeling, and I grabbed for her. Hands locked around each other's wrists, we fell down the rock face into the surging water.

My legs scraped across the rocks. A wave lifted me, slammed my shoulder into the rocks. My collarbone cracked. I gasped, gulping in water. Sea foam blinded me. I scrambled at the seaweed covered rocks, fingers slipping through masses of fragile sea lettuce. I caught a handful of razor-sharp wireweed and pulled my head free of the water for a split second. Seals, silver and black and beige, bobbed all around me.

"Mom!" Water filled my mouth again. A wave bashed me face-first into the rocks. Sleek furred heads butted me away from the rock. One of the seals swam between me and the rock, and I slammed into it, cushioned by its solid, blubbery body. I came up for air again, treading water with bloody feet and one arm. The seals' fishy breath and big eyes surrounded me. "Mom!"

"I'm here." She pulled me against her, one arm under my armpits. "Don't flail, puppy. I've got you." She towed me away from the crushing rocks. The seals swam with us, snorting and squealing. On the shore the fishermen were shouting. Their hands reached out to pull us in. One of them ran for blankets and towels from his trunk. Mom wrapped them around me and rubbed me down until I stopped shaking.

"Lady, you want me to call your husband?" one of them said. "There's a pay phone down the road."

"We're fine. Thank you." She pulled me up and made me walk to the car where I huddled in the passenger seat while she drove me to the hospital for x-rays.

When Dad came home from work and saw my face all scraped up and my shoulder in a brace he lost his mind. What happened? Was there an accident? Did you get the other driver's name?

"Leave her alone," Mom said. "It was my fault." He followed her into the kitchen demanding answers. What the hell were you thinking? Were you trying to get her killed? Maybe I should just sell the car and take your license, too. Is that what you want?

"Does it hurt real bad?" Caeli asked.

"Yeah."

"I could go get you some ice."

We both turned our eyes toward the kitchen. "It's not that bad."

Caeli hugged me and turned on the TV to *Bewitched* with the sound way up.

~ * ~

Dad left for another business trip the day after my shoulder brace came off.

"Don't forget your socks, Daddy," Caeli said from the couch as the cabman took his bags out to the car.

He laughed and gave us each a hug good-bye. Mom stood by the door to hand him his coat like she always did. He kissed her on the cheek.

"Good-bye. I love you."

"I love you too."

"Be good, kids!"

Instead of shutting the door behind him, Mom stood on the lintel watching him go. Her chest heaved as if she had been running a marathon. Her fist clenched, red nails digging into her palm. The cab disappeared around the corner and still she stood there watching.

"Mom, what are you doing?" Davy said.

She gasped, a sobbing gulp of air, and ran for her bedroom. We followed her, the younger ones trailing behind me. Hat boxes, winter sweaters, a shoe stretcher crashed to the floor as she flung things out of the closet. Dad's secret box. He'd finally left it behind.

Still breathing like she was drowning, Mom shoved past us, the box clenched in her hands. She smashed it against the counter until she was screaming and crying. The countertop was gouged and streaked.

She took a chef's knife and hacked at the box. It bent, but didn't open. She dug through the cupboard. Pots and pans clattered around the floor. "Where is it?" She pulled out the never-used cast iron frying pan someone had given her as a wedding present. Both hands wrapped around the handle, she smashed it down on the box. Her hands blistered where the iron touched her skin.

The lid cracked. The lock sprang open. Laughing, crying, gasping, she pulled out a seal skin. Not a seal costume or a piece of fur, but a whole skin slit down the front from chin to crotch as if someone had unzipped a seal and turned its skin into a onesie. It was silver and black, the face so perfectly preserved the whiskers trembled on the face. Only the eyes were missing. Mom sank to the floor, hugging it to her and rocking.

"Mom?" Caeli asked eventually. "Are we going to the beach?"

We didn't drive to the usual sandy beaches this time. Mom loaded us up in the convertible without a chance to gather our things and drove north up the PCH to the place where I had broken my shoulder. There weren't any fisherman today.

She led us back to the same rock where we had fallen in. First she hurled the broken box as far out into the water as she could. Then she hugged each one of us. She ran her fingers through our hair. She called us her puppies.

"I love you. I'm sorry."

Davy, fourteen-year-old Davy, started to cry. "What's going on? Mom what are you doing?"

She hugged him again, tears in her eyes. "I'm sorry. I'm so sorry. But I can't take you with me."

Then she jumped. No dramatic gesture. No explanations. She just jumped, wrapping the seal skin around her as she fell. Her great dark eyes showed once above the water, her tailfins flipped. She dove. None of us have seen her since.

~ * ~

She had left the keys in the car. There was money in her purse and food in the fridge. I didn't tell Dad anything until he came home a week later and found the trashed bedroom, the box missing.

When I graduated from high school, I don't know why, but I thought she might come. Show up in the middle of the crowd, head bobbing over the waves of hair for a second. She didn't.

When I married Roger, she didn't come to stop me. Nor when I divorced him four years later.

I like to think she made it all the way back to Ireland, swimming around the tip of South America and across the Atlantic. Or maybe she's as close as San Diego, and all I'd have to do is walk the beach at the right moment to find her sunning herself, eyes closed in bliss, flippers folded over her stomach.

~ * ~ * ~

Sarah Joy Adams writes female driven urban fantasy inspired by Celtic folklore and Norse family sagas. She is also a freelance editor and technical writer, but promises she is still fun at parties and never corrects people's grammar unless they ask first. She has lived in many different regions of the US, and recently settled in North Carolina, though she is still a New England Yankee at heart. She is the author of *Kinslayer Winter*, which was a finalist for the 2023 Manly Wade Wellman Award. Her other works include *Changeling's Fall, Winter's Heir*, and *Traitor's Spring,* all co-written with Emily Lavin Leverett. The fourth book in the series, *Summer's Regent,* is due out in 2024.

You can find her online at https://www.sarahjoyadams.com/, Facebook under her author name, and TikTok @changeling_writer.

OVER COFFEE

Teresa Milbrodt

The angels took their coffee black since that was the most saintly and pure, albeit bitter, way to drink the brew. Angels weren't supposed to need sugar and cream, though their eyes often darted to the condiments in the corner. I was surprised at their resolve, but angels were nothing if not controlled.

The fairy population that frequented my shop was much more relaxed in their choice of drinks, their language, and pretty much everything else, but they got along well with the angels and cracked jokes in the morning. The angels laughed, even at the dirty jokes. They never told that kind, though I could tell by the way they glanced at each other and smirked that they knew a fair share. The only other thing angels couldn't mention was jealousy, how the fairies got to have all the fun while angels had to comport themselves with care and not spill coffee on their robes, save the fallen ones who could laugh loudly and show their bra straps. We always had a few of those in the coffee shop. They ordered triple shots of espresso and poured in eight sugars.

Everyone sat at the same high tables and perched on the same wooden bar stools, though fairies and angels rarely mixed. It was easy to tell who was who from the unspoken dress code. The fairies wore sleeveless frocks that rarely fell below the knee, while I doubt I ever saw an angel's ankle or elbow. They could never agree on a musical selection—the fairies said Gregorian chants sounded like a dirge, while the angels said that fairy songs were as shrill as hyperactive hummingbirds—but nobody was happy when it was quiet. The wall decorations were a bit less controversial, since I'd hung up pictures of flowers: lotus, lily of the valley, poppies, and roses. It was harder to object to flowers, no matter the magical connotations and deno-tations and purported uses. The fairies were the main consumers of pastries and donuts, but sometimes eight angels would agree to split one powdered sugar donut, and eat while leaning forward so as to not get any sugar on their robes. I felt a certain amount of pride about bringing them all together, since when everyone left they smelled exactly the same.

But that was an earlier time, when humanity had split loyalties. Then, people prayed to angels and believed in fairies, expected demons in the forest and burned incense to ward off ghosts. I knew things would change—I couldn't have counted so many centuries in the business and not expected that—so I wasn't surprised when people lost their faith in fairies. Some even lost their belief in angels, but not as many. This left the morning angels to sip black coffee and try not to look smug, while the fairies lolled around all day, reading the paper and playing chess and checkers at the high tables and being snippy. They were able to linger over coffee and buy refills, glaring at the angels who were now answering their cell phones, being sent on this or that mission, and debating how many of them could fit on the head of a pin.

Since the fairies were still a large percentage of my clientele, I did my best to cheer them up.

"Just because you've lost a few believers doesn't mean you have to go into retirement," I said. "Nothing's stopping you from gadding about like you always did."

My optimism was greeted with a shrug.

"If no one appreciates our efforts," one fairy told me, "what's the point to good deeds or mischief?"

When the fairies had been in their heyday, they'd had a fine time tangling the hair of sleepers and stealing trinkets from night stands, leading travelers astray, and whisking away small children, leaving changelings in their place. People knew to pacify the fairies with offerings of bread and butter and cream, but now no one was even setting out old French fries and cold pizza. I could see where they'd get disheartened.

The fairies moped about, wondering aloud if they should find a new line of work or just retire, but most of them drank more coffee and kept grousing. After decades of such malaise, they'd become snarky and wizened. Even the fairies who'd been attractive and sprightly soon aged with boredom and moved slowly as if they'd become arthritic during these years of dismissal by humanity. When I suggested they could find part-time jobs, perhaps play with computer viruses or financial markets, they looked at me like I was daft. Once you've gone out of vogue in the mythological world, it's hard to stage a comeback.

I admit that I started the competitions, but it was to build the fairies' confidence and remind them that they still had certain powers due to their otherworldly status. I'd been sponsoring various coffee shop matches for years, and they were popular with my angel and fairy customers alike. Everything from cake generating to endangered species protection to oil baron annihilation—always a favorite when the competitors got creative.

But nothing quite matched the dream games.

From the beginning, the rules were few. The emotional reaction of the dreamer determined the winner. Said dreamer needed to cry in frustration when they awoke because the dream was so wonderful, or start battering the bedpost with a pillow because they thought their furniture had become a monster. For the first several dream competitions this guideline was upheld, but then the rules shifted.

I don't remember if it was an angel or a fairy who made the remark over morning coffee, how the stakes could be changed because we weren't really using the true power of dreams. Those nighttime illusions had always been portents of what was to come, visions or warnings of the future. Dreams were oracles imbued with meaning, rich with symbols, and the true test of a good dream creator was how that story might carry into the real world, changing the behavior of the dreamer during waking hours.

They started innocently enough with common folk, one angel against one fairy, each sending dreams that needed little imagination to interpret—the dreamers saw friends they hadn't spoken with in years and remembered to call when they woke up, made cookies and were prompted to bake in the morning, lost their dogs and remembered to check the leash twice before going out for a walk. Scoring was easy:

Would dreaming of owls make them study harder?

Would dreaming of dentures make them floss their teeth?

Would dreaming of poverty make them skip the morning latte?

But soon the fairy and angel contestants were sprinkling dreams on newscasters, television actresses, prominent lawyers, and others in the public spotlight. How could the dream toy with their language, raise their suspicions, redirect their reading? Could dreams change the stories they covered, roles they accepted, cases they took to court?

Post-dream debates became heated with caffeine and bravado.

The newscaster would not have spent so much time on the story about the children's hospital if she had not dreamed of her own daughter drowning the previous night. The actor would have accepted the bit part in that movie even if he hadn't dreamed of winning an academy award. The lawyer had obviously chosen to settle out of court because he'd dreamed of going bankrupt.

Each side promised that the next day their competitor would raise the stakes. I should not have been surprised when they started to create enigmatic dreams for superstitious world leaders, which included most all of them. Even if a politician entered high office with few such beliefs, the post bred its fair share of rituals and wariness.

One of the primary contenders in the dream battles was an angel who was known for going old-school, meaning Old Testament, meaning she had no qualms about doling out images of fire and brimstone and ash raining from the sky. I suppose once you'd witnessed something like that a few times you could get rather clinical about the whole affair and greet it with a shrug, and I thought the spectacle was rather passé, but it didn't stop her from reenacting her favorite fiery moments in dreams. I'm not sure what dream she granted a certain dictator, but two days later he ordered soldiers to ransack a village of innocents. The angels and fairies alike gasped as we watched the news reports. No one cast a glance in her direction. She wrinkled her nose and sighed.

"I'll look after them," she said, "resurrect the righteous from the ashes and such."

After that, everyone was a little nervous. They nodded quickly when I suggested another conceptual cake competition. They were too shaken to dabble in dreams for a while, but I knew they couldn't leave it alone forever.

The beneficence competition was more challenging. Not as many world leaders could be coerced into kindness, even if the dreams they received were overt about charity. The angels sent dreams of starving children standing in long soup kitchen lines, while the fairies sent dreams of bone-thin men working barren fields. A few of the dream-blessed leaders passed out corn to lines of starving subjects after they were threatened by images of a tidal wave overtaking the palace or mansion. It was discouraging to everyone in the coffee shop, knowing how severely you had to threaten kings with harm to their person or economic resources. The fairies were particularly blatant, sending phantoms of droughted crops and barren tourist attractions. Even then, so few leaders were willing to be kind.

The fairies spent long mornings moping over their mochas, complaining about the lack of generosity, but then they decided to take concrete action and make good on their dream promises. They were going to stick it to the misers, cause palace plumbing to go bad, walls to be cracked and overrun with invasive ivy, and rising tides to lick the foundations and make them threaten to crumble.

"We considered some good old-fashioned crop blights," one fairy told me. "Those were fun back in the day, but they harm the farmers more than the rulers. We have to be practical about this."

I was impressed, since fairies were rarely practical, but they felt better after the destruction of a few summer castles and allowing pirates to raid a couple of treasuries. It was invigorating to be active in the world again, even if no one realized they were causing the deviltry or left out potato chips to appease them. The fairies returned to plotting mischief over mochas, and the angels returned to black coffee and envy, rolling their eyes as we watched the evening news about the latest king who'd abdicated the throne to his son. Rumor had it he'd gone insane because of strange dreams, but doctors put him on medications and said he would be just fine after a year of treatment, counseling, and meditation. All the medical experts on the evening news agreed it would be wise for him to take a break, since the stress of the job must have gotten to him.

The fairies high-fived in the corner and the angels rolled their eyes, but because they were angels, they couldn't tell the fairies not to gloat. The fairies ordered pastries to celebrate, then clustered around a table to plan the next hidden revolution. So many countries, so many possibilities, so many new dreams to experiment with and see if they could set minds right. Perhaps it didn't compare to the immediate gratification of leading travelers astray or leaving changelings in cradles, but as the fairies giggled and slapped their knees, tittering over the next dream proposal, I was happy that they might have learned to adapt. Perhaps, given enough time, they would earn offerings of pizza and beer and chocolate cake after all.

~ * ~ * ~

Teresa Milbrodt is the author of three short story collections: *Instances of Head-Switching, Bearded Women: Stories,* and *Work Opportunities.* She has also published a novel, *The Patron Saint of Unattractive People,* and a flash fiction collection, *Larissa Takes Flight: Stories.* Her fiction, creative nonfiction, and poetry have appeared in numerous literary magazines. She earned her MFA in Fiction and MA in American Culture Studies from Bowling Green State University, and her PhD in English from the University of Missouri. She is addicted to coffee, long walks with her MP3 player, and writes the occasional haiku.

Dances with Elves

Cynthia Ward

"Elves!" called Rooso the Anvil. "O fair folk, hear my plea! I have given up my family and my trade! I have given up the human world! I want to join you!"

The fair folk were the greatest, purest, wisest people in the world. They lived in peace with one another, in accord with the spirits, and in harmony with nature. Where they lived, the forest bloomed all year with sweet-scented blossoms and sweet-tasting fruit. When they hunted, the animals came willingly to them. Sometimes, Rooso knew, they stole human babies. He did not understand why this caused the parents such sorrow; the elves had given the children a gift beyond compare.

Rooso the Anvil waited, but no answer to his call came from the surrounding forest. Finally he crouched, slowly, as though pressed down by the weight of the darkness around his small fire. Three nights and three days had he waited, alone in the wilderness, surviving on nuts and berries. He had brought no food into the forest and, though he was a blacksmith, he had brought no iron.

"Why couldn't I have been raised by the fair folk?" Rooso asked the night. He bowed his head. "O Gods," he prayed, "grant me my wish, to join the first and greatest of Your creations."

When he raised his head, he found his campfire ringed about by seven motionless elves. He had been accounted 'fair as an elf' by the women of his town, but in the presence of the elves he suddenly felt as ugly and gnarled as a hunchback.

The tallest of the tall elves spoke, in the Old Tongue, in a voice as clear and flowing as a stream. "We have heard your cries, these last three nights. Why do you disturb us?"

"I called you because I wish to join you." Rooso heard his voice creak like an old chair, but made himself continue. "I have left the world behind, in pursuit of my desire. You are so wise and fair, I would give anything to be one of you."

The elves smiled at one another, a brief flash of teeth whiter than a human smile could ever be.

The tallest elf turned back to Rooso. "If you are willing, human, you may become one with the elves."

"You *know* I am willing."

"I am known as Eagle Striking," said the tallest elf. "Put out your fire, human, and follow us."

Rooso emptied his waterskin, extinguishing the small fire. He blinked in the blackness of night.

~ * ~

At dawn, the elves led the human out of the forest, into a clearing overgrown with wild roses, strawberries, poppies, daisies, and a score of flowers Rooso did not recognize. In the middle of this field stood a grove of fruit and oak trees. The apple, pear, and cherry trees were bowed under the weight of fruit. The elves dwelt high in the branches of the oaks, in shelters woven of branches and grass. Among the several score elves who greeted him, Rooso saw a few children, all as quiet, dignified, and beautiful as the adults. He saw no human children. If there were changelings here, they had changed completely.

The fair folk prepared a feast of welcome. Some piled wood high in the center of the grove, while others filled baskets with fruit and berries. Eagle Striking led Rooso out of the grove and deeper into the ancient forest. He bade Rooso stand quiet in the shadow of a shaggy pine. Then he drew his knife. Rooso's heart slammed against his chest. Eagle Striking turned away.

The elf took up a position several yards from Rooso. He stood motionless, his white skin and butter-colored buckskin tunic shading into the browns and yellows of tree boles and fallen leaves.

Within moments a red deer appeared, a great stag crowned with tined antlers. Head upraised, legs steady, the stag approached the elf and stretched out its slender neck. Eagle Striking laid the stone knife across the jugular and sawed at the tough hide. When blood spurted like water from a fountain, Rooso felt faint, though he had poached the king's deer many times. He reminded himself that the animal had come to Eagle Striking in accord with the harmony of nature.

At the feast, Rooso the Anvil ate better than he ever had in his life. The venison was savory, not gamy, and tender as veal. As the feast progressed, a group of elves chanted wild, strange songs Rooso couldn't understand over the bone-shaking throb of log drums.

When other elves rose up and made a ring around the fire, Rooso realized he was about to witness the legendary dance of the elves. He could not believe his good fortune. He never expected to be invited to join them.

He shook his head at their beckoning gestures until Eagle Striking left the dance and grabbed his wrist and dragged him to the fire. "Human, do you see the pattern?"

Rooso shook his head. The pattern was far too complex and the drumming too fast. But the beat slowed, and the dancers shouted encouragement, and moved slowly so he could learn. Eagle Striking pulled him into motion, and the drums beat fast again, and Rooso found himself dancing the ancient Elvish dance.

~ * ~

In the morning, Rooso ate as well as he had last night, break-fasting on fruit, wild-pig ham, and wheat bread dipped in honey. He lay against a tree, his hands on his overfull stomach, somnolent, insensible of the passing hours.

Eagle Striking came up to him and pressed a scrap of dried fruit into his hand.

"I am not hungry," Rooso said apologetically.

"Eat this toadstool if you would see as we see," Eagle Striking said. "Eat, and know the harmony of the world."

Rooso examined the toadstool, a long, dirty-looking white stem topped with a small, tight-fitting brown cap. How could this shriv-eled scrap give him the wisdom of elves?

He felt his stomach tremble. He quickly thrust the mushroom into his mouth and bit down. The stem snapped like an old stick. As he chewed, his saliva softened the mushroom, but the foul taste blotted up the moisture in his mouth. He swallowed with difficulty. He could not imagine how he could gain knowledge in this manner, and the attempt to imagine it made his stomach queasy. He calmed his mind and lay still.

After a while he realized the trees of the grove made a pattern. The pattern included all the trees he could see, and all the trees he could not see. He understood the pattern of the forest: the harmony of the trees with the animals, with the birds that flew above, with the worms that burrowed below. He understood the necessity of the deer eating the leaves and the wolf eating the deer. He turned to look at the huge oak he leaned against, and traced the furrows in the bark, following the pattern. *Everything* was part of the pattern. Rooso the Anvil laid his cheek against the rough bark, spread his arms as wide as they could stretch, and embraced the tree.

When evening thickened in the grove, the Elves built their bonfire. The human stared into the fire, watching the flames leap and twist in a dance as beautiful and meaningful as the dance of the Elves, or the pattern of the world.

Rooso realized Eagle Striking stood beside him, and the other Elves stood close around him. Eagle Striking laid his hand gently on Rooso's shoulder. "Human, do you see the pattern?"

Rooso spoke slowly. "Yes."

Eagle Striking asked, "Are you ready to be one with the elves?"

Rooso smiled dreamily. "I am," he replied.

And so the Elves cooked and ate him.

~ * ~ * ~

Cynthia Ward (http://www.cynthiaward.com) has published stories in *Analog*, *Asimov's*, *Nightmare*, *Weird Tales*, and elsewhere. She is the editor of *Lost Trails: Forgotten Tales of the Weird West: Volumes 1-2* and a co-editor of *Weird Trails*. With Nisi Shawl, she co-created Writing the Other, which received the Locus Special Award in 2020. *The Adventure of the Golden Woman* (Aqueduct Press) concludes Cynthia's Blood-Thirsty Agent series. She lives in Los Angeles, where she is not working on a screenplay.

The Magic in the Melody

Shayna Coplan

Little winged fairies taught Arnold to play the guitar when he was very young. They loved the sweet notes that fell from the strings, but were too small to manipulate the instrument themselves. Arnold wasn't special—it was just that his house was built near the undergrowth and stream the fairies used to travel between worlds. They might have taught his sister, but her window didn't face the right direction. The same two fairies waited every night for Arnold's parents to slip into dreaming. They put the guitar into his small hands and showed him how to pluck the strings. They cast a spell to keep the music bouncing around the walls of his bedroom, never to leak out into the world. They even spelled each of his parents into thinking the other had purchased the rosewood guitar.

Arnold grew some, and began taking lessons from the old jazz musician who lived with his daughter down the street. The fairies were jealous at first, but they quieted once Arnold showed them the new sounds he could coax from the guitar.

One summer evening, he returned home to find the two fairies sitting on his bed with crossed arms and raised eyebrows. It reminded him of the time he'd broken curfew and found his parents waiting on the couch. Arnold leaned his guitar case against his dresser and stood in front of the tiny figures.

"What?" he finally asked when he couldn't take their silence any longer.

The one called Serra stood on his bedspread and launched herself into the air. Her wings moved so quickly they disappeared and a distant hum tickled Arnold's ear. Serra hovered only inches from his face and pointed a tiny finger at his nose.

"You played a concert for the mortals!"

Arnold's mouth fell open. "I would call it a recital, but yeah," he answered.

Serra threw her arms in the air and her dress made of butterfly wings sprouted a tiny tear. "Your music belongs to us! How dare you share it with strangers so freely."

Arnold struggled not to cover his ears. Her yelling sounded like breaking glass.

"My music doesn't belong to anyone, not even me," he argued.

She continued as if he hadn't spoken, "If you play a concert for the mortals, don't you think it's only fair that you play a concert for us?"

"I play concerts for you every night," he said. In fact, his grades were starting to suffer from the lack of sleep.

"That's different. Those are your lessons. We need a proper concert in our own lands."

The other fairy didn't typically agree with Serra, but this time he nodded enthusiastically. Arnold had done his research when he was old enough to realize nightly visits from fairies were not normal. He'd read the stories and knew to tread lightly.

"But you live in fallen trees and mushrooms. How am I to play a concert there?" he asked.

The fairies laughed in unison and the sound made muscles low in Arnold's abdomen tighten. Tin, the male fairy, stood up and walked to the edge of the blankets.

"Our home is in the between places. The fallen logs and green things are only the doors. There are ways of ushering mortals through for a time."

Tin and Serra flew to the windowsill and together they carried a leaf back to Arnold. Inside the leaf was a pink liquid with blues and greens playing on the surface like an oil slick. Tin lifted his side toward Arnold.

"You will drink this and come with us."

"And if I refuse?" Arnold asked. You weren't supposed to drink anything given to you by fairies and you certainly weren't supposed to follow them home. Time moved differently there, and an hour spent with them might be twenty years in the mortal realm. At least, that's what the books in the library said.

"You will drink this or we will take the music from you," Serra answered quietly.

Arnold took a step back. "You can't do that."

"Any gift that is ours to give is also ours to rescind. You may start as a beginner again, but you'll find your fingers too clumsy and the notes bent before they meet your ear."

Arnold tried to imagine his life without the guitar and couldn't.

It was as much a part of him as his liver or kidneys.

"Can I say goodbye to my parents first?" he asked.

Serra rolled her sky-colored eyes. "There's no need for dramatics. I promise you safe return."

Arnold nodded and waited for the sick feeling to leave his throat before parting his lips for the fairies. The small figures carefully angled the leaf toward his mouth.

"Wait!" Tin called.

Arnold paused with the leaf touching his bottom lip. He hoped that Tin had a change of heart and might convince his friend.

"You need to be holding your guitar."

Tin left Serra holding the leaf by herself and brought the instrument to Arnold. He had never seen Tin wear a shirt, only pants seemingly sewed from the petals of dark blue flowers. Still, even though he was used to the small fairy's rippling muscles, it was amazing to watch a six-inch figure fly with a full-sized guitar dangling from his grip.

The pink liquid tasted like the forest floor smelled. One instant Arnold was standing in his bedroom gripping his guitar and the next he was falling. Colors, sounds and shapes melted together until they became impossible to understand. Arnold tasted purple and heard a triangle. Panic galloped through his chest and he felt an immense pressure on his skull.

Arnold landed on his butt and his guitar fell heavily into his lap a moment later. Tin offered him a hand up and Arnold was amazed to find the small fairy was actually several inches taller than him.

"Sorry. Traveling by shadows can be jarring the first time," Tin said as he lifted Arnold to his feet. Even Tin's voice was deeper here.

They were in a bustling city formed from growing things. Living trees grew into the shapes of buildings. Soaring redwoods formed skyscrapers and willows made small, squat homes. The road was made from smooth river rocks and tall braided grasses formed fences.

"It's beautiful," Arnold said.

Fairies walked purposefully past them, some carried bags woven from moss while others chatted with squirrels and rabbits that came nearly to their shoulders. Arnold couldn't decide if the fairies were small or the rodents were large. Serra pulled him by the hand impatiently.

"Of course it is. New is often beautiful, except for when it's scary." A fairy child stopped to stare at Arnold's wingless back and nearly fell when he started forward again. A tree branch swept in from above and righted the child before he could scrape a knee.

Now that Serra stood only a few inches shorter than him he noticed her deeply tanned skin and full bottom lip. He'd always thought of the fairies as childlike because of their size, but he realized how wrong he'd been. Arnold's hand began to sweat where it rested in her smaller palm. He tried not to look when the sunbeams turned her delicate orange and black dress nearly transparent.

They halted in front of a building formed by a twisted olive tree.

"You can warm up before the concert begins. We will gather everyone," she said. Serra gave him a gentle push toward the door and Arnold nearly fell into the concert hall. The space was much larger than it appeared on the outside. Hundreds of seats were formed from individual bushes with wide, waxy leaves. The seats sloped up so that everyone might see the gnarled wood stage.

"Hello?" he called. No one answered.

Arnold paced the stage in front of the hummingbird-feather curtain and wondered which songs to play. It was probably best to stick to the melodies the fairies had taught him, but he couldn't resist throwing in something better suited to a smoky jazz hall.

His fingers warmed the guitar's neck as the music filled the empty space. The open roof let in plenty of sunlight, but Arnold preferred playing among shadows. Maybe it was all of the lessons in the dead of night, but he thought melodies floated through darkness best. As if spurred by his thought, the branches above knitted together to block out the sun. It was too dark to see the guitar in his lap and an uneasy feeling filled him.

"Hello?" he called again, ashamed at the tremble in his voice.

The only answer was a buzzing sound as a thousand fireflies danced in from an open window. They covered the ceiling with their swooping embers and filled the hall with the perfect glow of a well-placed fire.

"Thank you," Arnold said. Was there a fairy lighting tech out there, or was he thanking the tree itself? It didn't much matter.

Tin and Serra returned a short while later and ushered him behind the curtain. The sound of the growing audience comforted Arnold. They sounded just like a human audience.

The curtain parted and Arnold took a few unsteady steps toward the single chair shaped bush on the stage. A cluster of fireflies dislodged from the group and created a spotlight by flying in slow circles above his head. The first few notes were uncertain and he sensed uncomfortable restlessness from the audience. Arnold paused, took a deep breath and pretended he was sitting on his bed while Tin and Serra danced in the air above his dresser. The calming technique sent a bolt of longing through him, and he focused the sad energy through his guitar.

The audience erupted in applause and hollers as he finished the first song. The next was an upbeat ditty that forced his guitar to sound more like a fiddle. Dozens of fairies lifted from their seats and started twisting and diving through the air. Arnold's fingers raced along the fret at a manic speed. He'd read about fairy dancing. It could get so frenzied that a mortal would die of exhaustion before thinking of quitting. Was his playing like that now? Would the friction from his plucking create a flame that would consume him before he even tried to push the instrument away?

He played like that for hours. Arnold didn't die, but by the end his fingers were bloody and the muscles of his forearms were cramped.

Arnold waited for Serra to finish rubbing a balm onto his hands that made the pain disappear completely.

"Can I go home now?" he asked.

Serra only rubbed more of the rose smelling lotion into his skin and wouldn't meet his eyes. Arnold looked to Tin for an answer.

"You played longer than we expected. Mortals can only travel by shadows when the stars are in the right place. We can't leave tonight," Tin said quietly.

"But I have to get back home!" His parents would be crushed by his disappearance. How much time had already passed while he'd played their stupid concert?

"Nature has laws even in this place, and they will not be broken," Serra explained with a shrug.

Days of waiting turned to weeks and the weeks into months. Arnold moved into the apartment Tin shared with his brother. He tried to buy some of the shadow potion on his own, but none of the shop owners would sell to a human. Arnold begged Serra and Tin to return him home, but they only told him to be patient and changed the subject quickly.

How much time had passed at home? A year? Ten years? Twenty? Every time Arnold fell too deeply into the depths of memory and longing the fairies pulled him back out. They distracted him with new clothes spun from spider's webs or got him a pet slug to occupy his time.

Arnold's guitar lessons continued with the best musicians in that slice of reality. He played until his fingers bled because it was the only thing that sounded like home. And because their elixirs could heal blisters and make an ache disappear in an instant.

He sat on the dirt floor of Tin's apartment watching a fairy named Blossom show him a progression. Every chord she played was executed perfectly, but it sounded cold and unfeeling.

"Your playing sounds different than mine," Arnold finally said, choosing his words carefully.

Blossom didn't even look up from her instrument. "Of course it does."

"Why?"

Instead of addressing his question, she asked her own, "How do you feel?"

Arnold considered lying to be polite, but he turned to the truth. "Lonely. You are all very kind, but I miss home. I miss my parents. And I'm angry. I feel like a prisoner and it's not fair."

She nodded. "I can hear the darkness in your music. You humans feel everything so deeply. It makes the music an expression of something more than just the manipulation of strings at different levels of tension. It's really the only magic your kind has."

"You don't feel things?" he asked.

Blossom finally looked up. "Fairies are nearly always content with the exception of fleeting, petty moments. There is the occasional jealousy or pang of fear, but they are forgotten and forgiven very quickly."

"That sounds…nice," Arnold answered. Contentment sounded better than the constant churning in his own gut.

"Perhaps. But at its core music is about love. It might be requited love, or lost love, or the love of a place, but it's always about love."

"And fairies don't love?"

She leaned her snail-shell guitar carefully against the wall. "We like everyone and everything, but I'm not sure we love. By the same token, we don't hate either."

Arnold shook his head. "I'm not sure the human way is better."

Blossom shrugged and then stilled, tilting her head like a curious dog. Serra and Tin walked in a moment later and stood over Arnold grinning.

"Are you ready to go home?" Tin asked.

"Yes!" Arnold shouted, and scrambled to his feet. But doubt tickled the corners of his mind by the time he was standing. He couldn't be sure that home wouldn't be less familiar now than the land of the fairies.

Serra put a small hand on his shoulder. "You are welcome here any time. You can even stay if you'd like," she told him.

Arnold considered staying. His heart pounded with the knowledge that every minute of hesitation the world spun further from his time. His parents would be older, with heavily lined faces. Maybe his father's hypertension had finally caught up with him. Or they would all be dead, and he'd find himself a stranger among flying cars and holograms.

Still, it only took him a few minutes to decide to go home. The falling was easier the second time. The shadows were made from pieces of both worlds and Arnold had spent enough time in each.

He landed on his bed, surprised to see the same posters on the wall. Had his parents kept it as a shrine to their missing son? Arnold paused at the half-finished glass of water he'd left on his nightstand before the recital all those months ago. It was still there. He took a sip and didn't even taste dust.

Arnold took the stairs two at a time and found his parents settling on the couch in front of the television.

"So, you do want dinner then?" his mother asked. He'd turned down the stew months prior. Arnold crossed the room in three steps and wrapped his arms around his mother. She returned his hug after a stiff moment of surprise.

Tin and Serra were waiting for him when he went back upstairs to his room. It was odd to be towering over them once again.

"I thought years would have passed. I didn't think I'd still have a home."

Serra's tiny eyebrows cinched and she put a hand on her hip. "Barely five minutes have passed in this realm. Do you think we would steal time from you in that way?"

Arnold could only shrug and hope she didn't notice his embarrassed flush. "The stories all say that you do."

Tin snorted. "Stories written by jealous humans who did not earn the favor of entering our lands. You've stolen nearly a year more of life."

Arnold tried desperately to do the trans-reality math. "Wait, does that mean all the hours you've spent in my room were years rolling by in your own world?"

Tin nodded. "It's true we've lost decades, but I'd happily trade them again to hear you play. Maybe now you see why we are protective of your gifts."

Tin and Serra waved goodbye and jumped into the shadows.

The next day, Arnold sat in a chair across from the old jazz musician, who fanned himself and said, "Boy, you've been holding back on me!"

After that, the fairies had to be content in sharing Arnold with the world, because music is a lot like time—it doesn't belong to anyone.

~ * ~ * ~

Shayna Coplan is a middle school history and creative writing teacher in southern California. She spends most of her waking hours gleefully outnumbered by adolescents, and uses the accompanying insanity to fuel her fiction. You can experience some of the madness at www.twitter.com/CoplanShayna

silver and scythe

Manny Frishberg and Edd Vick

Fenod grumbled to himself and slapped cold hands to colder arms. "A brownie am nae meant to slog through half-frozen mud," he grumbled.

King Pellaidh, as grimy as his elderly servant, looked up through a patch of flowers to where a party of Elves sat mounted on pristine stags.

"All the fey races are here represented," he said. "We kings had to ensure the council of war was in a spot equally as distasteful to all." A faint burst of laughter came on the wind. "But hark, the scouts return."

Sweeping into the camp, a trio of blue fairies spun to a halt. The wind that carried them died in a patter of clods and leaves. Their leader brandished his spear.

"It is true!" he said. "The humans make iron."

"Aye, for weapons nae doubt," Fenod muttered. All present knew the metal was a mortal poison to their kind. His sentiment echoed among the assembled spirits.

"Not proven," Crom Cruaich.said. The crook-backed god lifted his head as high as it would reach. "Not even alleged yet," he shouted to be heard over the throng.

Queen Medbh gathered her robes, the color of the sky just before first light, and stood up from her throne, blonde braids held in place by a chased gold band around her forehead. "Then let the fairies speak."

"They have melted the stones and seen fire pour in yellow rivulets," said Aelfric, spearing the air with his fine silver lance for emphasis.

"The Sons of Mil gathered the black branches when the light died and they cooled," Hefeydd said. His pale blue eyes grew wide with unfamiliar dread.

Kheelan straightened to his full twelve hands and waited. All around, the sidhe and fair folk looked from one to another. Water sprites gurgled softly from their brook. The elves's steeds shuffled nervously in the stillness.

"They fashion knives from metal," he said, "and they make axe-heads."

"Weapons!" several said.

"They're baneful vipers," shouted an elf.

"Kill them all," yelled a nearby kelpie, transforming in her anger from horse to shaggy dark-haired maiden and back.

Pellaidh leaped onto a hummock. "Wait," he said. "Knives and axes may have peaceful purposes. Do we not eat with silver knives?"

"Some of us do," Fenod muttered.

"Do we not fell trees and shape our houses with axes?"

There was a murmur, more of dissent than approval, among those present. Many sidhe lived wild, and most avoided any contact with the invaders. What commerce the fair folk did have with the mortals were with hapless boys who were led to *Tirn Aill*, or maidens snatched away to *Tir Tairngire*, the Plain of Happiness, then back in their beds before dawn. Pellaidh's people, alone among the Tuatha Dé, had regular contact with the newcomers. The Gruagach, brownies, found the mortals entertaining and, on occasion, Fenod or his brethren would ease their toil as they quaffed the milk the humans left for them.

"What would you have us do?" said Queen Medbh. "We and the Children of Mil have coexisted for aeons—but uneasily. We elves and sidhe have our gifts, but we are few beside these humans. If they are forging iron weapons, we must strike soon or see our lands and lives taken from us. So again I ask: what would you?"

All regarded the brownie king. His voice low, he said, "Consult Frige."

"Frige," said one, then it passed all around the gathering, "Frige." It was a beckoning, a plea more than a command. "Frige."

A tall, lithe woman appeared then and glided through the crowded spirits. All bowed deeply as she passed to the center of the throng. The ancient goddess surveyed her kith with patient resolve.

"We endure," she said, her voice a flowing stream over smooth stones. "The Milesians have been among us long enough for us to see what frail wisps they are, like dust in a fairy horde's wake. They live a short while, then return to the surrounding earth."

One of those gathered, feeling emboldened, spoke up. "What challenge does the wind face from a dust mote? What are men? A gall on a leaf hanging off a branch of the Great Tree."

"And yet," said the goddess, "where a single mote of dust is beneath our notice, massed into a plain of mud they drag us down." Frige spread her arms and turned her face toward King Pellaidh, and a golden beam connected them. "Are they dust?" she asked. "Or mire? Are they stone?"

"Truly, goddess, I do not know."

"The sidhe are not lightly called to war." Frige lowered her hands, one now holding an arrow, the other a feather. "Sound out their nature, and answer like with like." And then she was gone.

Everyone looked at King Pellaidh again. They had no doubt who was assigned the task.

"Blood and thunder," said Fenod. "A quest."

"You have a week," Crom Cruaich said.

The business settled, several broke out their harps and silver whistles, drums and uilleann pipes, filling the glade with riotous melodies. Dancers circled in the meadow, tall fairy princes clutching the hands of gnarled leprechauns, spinning water sprites spraying a fine mist, tinkling with their laughter.

~ * ~

The gray light of just-before-dawn stirred Fenod from his dreams. He blinked, still groggy from too much Fairy mead. He knew better than to quaff a hornful, but he also knew he would be dispatched to seek out the Sons and Daughters of Mil's true intent, so it would be days before he had another taste.

Pellaidh sat under a tree, already dressed in his travelling clothes, a tawny green tunic with a sash of oak leaves, an oaken scabbard topped by the hilt of his silver pommel and grip, slung low on his hip, his brown acorn cap tugged down almost covering his right eye.

"Time you were up, Fen," he said, rousing the aging servant with a slap to his rump. "Prepare to end humanity, or save it."

Fenod glared at the sound of his king's far-too-fervent humor as the sun crested the horizon. "Oh, my old bones," he said pulling himself erect. The rest of the fair folk lay in sodden stupors. "Ready, sire," he said.

Pellaidh whistled up a pair of trout in the river nearby and sat himself astride the larger one. Fenod was grateful his laird would not subject his head to a lengthy walk. He clambered aboard a feisty overweight fish. But their steeds's frequent exuberant leaps shortly robbed Fenod of his optimism.

Far inland, they left the fish in a bywater and, a league on from the stream, the pair crossed a bridge, imperceptible to the Sons and Daughters of Mil, into their realm and time.

Fenod and his laird crept through the open field of grasses. The old retainer licked his lips when he saw a pair of cows switching their tails near one of the huts. But, instead of gathering wild fruits or going off in hunting parties as they always had, the Children of Mil engaged in a new occupation.

As the brief human days unwound, some poked sticks in the ground, gouging long rows through the sod, tearing up Earth Mother's hair in clumps. As nights followed days before the fay watchers, men and women came back along, casting handfuls of wild barley corns onto the tortured ground. Plants took root and tiny flower sprites woke and danced around the ripening seed heads while the corns grew fat on their tall, stalky limbs. Fenod and Pellaidh laughed at the antics of the little plant spirits.

"Human ways are strange," Pellaidh said. "Yet, they do no real harm that I can see."

By now the human sun was racing along its arcing path faster, the moon rising and setting both in the darkness. Pellaidh, grinning, pointed to an earthenware bowl set outside a house's door.

"Milk, I'd wager," he said. They skulked closer and feasted on the offering left them.

Then, the humans committed an inexplicable horror—returning to the field with curved iron blades, they swept across the plain, slicing through the narrow stems, oblivious to the panicked screams of the barley sprites.

Pellaidh turned away from the scene of slaughter, but Fenod forced himself to watch. He gaped with a rising sense of dread as the narrow stalks were felled. The fragile spirits that inhabited them were torn in twain by the black metal blades. He watched their essences drift up to the clouds and wondered if they were returning to Elfhame or dispersing like motes of dust to fall to the ground like mortal things.

Eventually, the human sun fell below the far edge of the earth and their foul occupation was done for the time. The king and his retainer watched their departure from the killing fields with a boiling rage for these intruders, their offerings of milk be cursed.

"I have nae need to watch these creatures for even one of their short evenings more," said Fenod, kneeling.

His king stood silent, bent over by grief, still refusing to face the ground where the sprites had so recently cavorted. Creases of caring strained his face. The fay sun fell toward the Earth, bathing the shorn ground first with shimmering gold, darkening to red, then indigo, recounting the tragedy in the theater of colors. Were they humans, they would have cried.

When the curtain of night had fallen, King Pellaidh bade his servant away and they marched back to the fay bridge, shrouded in a cloak of silence. At the brookside the laird summoned their fishy steeds again and they rode through the fairy night to report the horror they had observed.

They arrived, by their own time, not much after the assembly had risen from another night of folly. A few elves and darker sorts of sidhe who favored the nighttime languished, but the major share of the Tuatha Dé Danaan were breaking their fasts with nectar and ambrosia, still harmonizing with airs played through the long night.

Crom Cruaich noticed the travelers first. The elder sidhe fell quiet as he caught sight of King Pellaidh, whose face still wore its stricken look.

"What news do our scouts bring of the Milesians? Are they of a peaceful bent, despite their truck with the black metal?" He spoke with the hopefulness that had carried the day before the pair left, though his reading of the Gruagach laird's countenance already told him all he needed to know. Queen Medbh, herself of a more bloodthirsty bent, grinned darkly.

Pellaidh squared his shoulders, composed his features, and simply said, "Humans kill our kind, I know not why, and they do it with iron." Fenod helped him to the place they had used before, and settled him on his hummock.

Some few younger Sidhe turned one to another inquiring what killing was, but all elder Tuatha Dé did not. They had fought the Firbolg, who had held these lands from time immemorial, and the Fomorian giants. Elfhame had gathered to its shores more than a few fallen fay in those battles.

"War." The chant started low, from the cu sith, the eaches, and other such fierce tribes. It was taken up by elves, by kelpies, and grew.

"War." Medbh raised her arms, her green eyes darkening, while Cruaich lowered his head, his heavy brows beetling.

"War."

Medbh turned once more to the assembled fair folk and silenced the mob with a gesture. "Are there any among you who cry peace?" Not a voice replied. "Then war it shall be! Gather your tribes at Magh Tuireadh."

Word went out by runners and riders on fishes and forest creatures, on the waves and the wind. Silver pikes caught the glint of the sun as they swirled up in the fairy wind, and stone battle axes swung from their hips as they rode and walked, swam and flew. The warrior throng assembled, readying itself to march on the human settlements.

On the other side of the veil of time, human seasons passed in the course of a fay day. The Children of Mil multiplied in their brief moments in the sun, grew tall, aged and died, but their numbers always increased, like their aurochs and goats, cattle and sheep spreading over the hills. They tore up longer and wider fields to seed with grains, and the Tuatha Dé heard the plaintive cries of the plant spirits each time they were felled. The lament made the blood turn cold in their veins but it sharpened their resolve as they hurried forth to battle.

Crom Cruaich beckoned Pellaidh and his vassal. "My kin, the brownies," he said, "Think you that, mounted on rabbits or foxes, you could be our scouts? None of us know the human lands as well as you."

Pellaidh nodded. "You may count on us."

~ * ~

Pellaidh and his small force of brownies sat their mounts ahead of the horde, watching the settlement sleep. They rode, splitting up as they traveled. Dawn's earliest light found them in the foothills, where they encountered their first surprise. Pellaidh's fox and Fenod's badger both shied away from the smell of humans far sooner than the Brownies had expected. They stared in amazement at a wide road made of beaten dirt, its center paved with worked stone. Looking uphill, they saw a great wound in the side of the mountain.

"They are quarrying," said Pellaidh. "But who could need so

much stone?"

"I'd need that much if I were commemorating every step I took," said his companion, nodding to the road.

Pellaidh shook his head, then turned his fox's head away from the quarry. "Our answers lie downhill."

They rode, not on the paved way and not even on the dirt bordering it, but in the forest to one side, riding quickly, dodging trees, heeding birdcalls and fairycalls, smelling the freshness of spring.

Barely half a human morning was gone when they saw a large agglomeration of stone buildings, a henge of tree trunks at its center. A bell tolled.

"Firbolg's Teeth," said Fenod. "These Sons and Daughters of Mil certainly can multiply."

"And build." Pellaidh's jaw was set. "This will not be so easy a nut to crack. Come, we report."

Fenod's badger, unused to long journeys, sighed as they turned about.

~ * ~

Queen Medbh declared the need for a war council and runners went through the camp, calling out those fay who had battled at Mag Tuireadh uncounted millennia past, to aid in planning a strategy. She led them across the bridge of time to where the humans dwelt in their brief allotment.

"For too many centuries our battles have been festive events, tournaments to display our bravery and practice skills long past the needing," she told the most elder of the assembled elves, fairies, and assorted tribes. "Now we must recall the days when we made war for the right to this land, for things have come to that turn again."

"Our jousts may be but jest these days," said Crom Cruaich, "but these silver lances we carry can still win the day." He brandished a finely chased silver spear, as delicate as lace and sharp as obsidian, that glistened in the moonlight. Another hoisted his battle axe high to catch the reflected light from Crom Cruaich's spearhead, and send it dancing on to an elfin sword swinging wildly, slicing through the cool night air.

"Enough," shouted Pellaidh. "We don't lack mettle—it is a plan we need."

At that the crowd settled down and the brownie laird drew the human villages as he had seen them last. In the truncated Milesian night, they drew out lines of attack, rubbed them into the dirt and retraced new lines until, in the last fading starlight, they had a strategy all could agree on.

The Fay horde crossed into the human realm when the moon was new and the night so dark that even a fox could not see its own feet. In the western mountains they formed their ranks, the fairy archers to the rear, bucca in front wielding their picks and stone hammers the size of a giant's fist, a legion of elves and other fay in the center hoisting their pikes and battle axes, dirks and broadswords above their heads.

Fenod felt a chill pass down his back when he thought of the upcoming battle. His king was young enough to have seen only the last of the battle against the giants of Fomor, when fay forces were in the ascendant. The elder brownie remembered darker, more uncertain days. Then he thought of how few humans there were, how weak they were without magic, and was cheered. How could the Tuatha Dé not carry the day? He looked to King Pellaidh, barely visible with the glamour on him.

Pellaidh's voice came. "Look there, 'tis the signal." And when Fenod turned, he saw a shining arrow head appear far overhead, produced with elvish magic. "Let us go," said the King, and though he spoke calmly his words carried easily to all brownie ears.

They attacked at night, and chose the first town Pellaidh and Fenod had found, a middling-sized place, as their target. A river passed through it, the better for water-dwellers to use in their assault. Pellaidh and his kin led the queen's forces to vantage points and to roads that would be blocked, while other, more ferocious fay silenced humans at farms, inns, and other outlying dwellings. The merest sliver of a moon looked down as a fir darrig and a brace of kelpies slew the guards at the town's main gate from behind. Then the main force of Fairyland swept down to dash through streets soon brimming in blood. Not a human was left alive. Magic and fine senses aided the fay in seeking them out to the last man, woman, and child.

Fenod and his liege stood on a hillside overlooking the town at daybreak. They had not seen most of the slaughter, being assigned as couriers and scouts, but now they could both see and smell it.

Pellaidh shivered, almost as if he had awoken from a nightmare.

"I like this not," he said. "I thought I had a stomach for battle, but this is butchery."

"Is it not necessary? You saw with your own eyes what the Children of Mil do to our kin."

"They killed Sprites, 'tis true. Yet they've never harmed a brownie, nor an elf, nor any other. Truth be told, I simply do not understand them."

"So far, so true." Fenod plucked a blade of grass as long as his forearm, first making sure it hosted no fairy. "Excepting for Sprites with the misfortune to be born only to be reaped."

"As we have gleaned here, this night past. And like these mortal interlopers, they are cursed to see but a scant few days before their time expires, while we watch the ebb and flow of time's tides."

"Aye." Now Fenod, too, felt a shudder pass through him. "But what alternative do we have? Stand with the humans? I think nay."

"I am no traitor," said Pellaidh. "Yet I feel there must be a third way between total peace and utter war. The horn. We are called."

Queen Medbh assembled the other sovereigns in the dale just past the bridge tween lands. "Fine sport, this," she said. Her auburn hair matched the gore she'd squelched underfoot. "And only three Tuatha Dé killed, all by their accursed iron weapons." She turned her face westward, watching a human day pass, then another. "Let us away, and kill again."

The sidhe assembled their ranks on her order and crossed the barrier between their realm and the humans' to march on the next settlement and drive the Children of Mil back across the sea. The night was barely half spent in the human lands when fairy archers lined the hill overlooking a small village, barely more than a rough circle of stone huts, thin trails of wood smoke rising from their thatched roofs.

Squat elves raised their shields of copper and their silver-bladed war axes, while swarms of other fair folk gathered clan by clan in squared-off rows, ready to charge into the gap at the call of trumpets. On a signal from the queen, horns blasted and the hordes of immortals streamed down the hill into the undefended village.

Except the village was not undefended. At first the Tuatha Dé met no resistance as they ran toward the central square—barely more than a patch of tamped-down earth filling the space between huts.

But as they found themselves confounded by the absence of enemies to slaughter, humans came streaming out their doors, screaming cries so shrill and wild they rivaled even the Ban Sidhe's wailing. In answer to the clamorous call more humans, as many as a field has flowers, ran at the archers from behind. They had smeared their skins with sap and mud to baffle the attackers' senses.

Into the fray the Sons and Daughters of Mil carried whatever they had at hand. Some struck the immortals with wooden pitchforks and cudgels, causing the elves to roar with laughter. But others wielded metal implements—butchering knives and hatchets for chopping kindling, scythes and shears that cut through fay bodies, leaving a trail of carnage in their wakes. In much less than a human hour the queen called a retreat and the fair folk withdrew to behind the veil between worlds.

Amid the keening for lost kin, the queen sought out King Pellaidh. "Speak to me of these humans. Our second attack was on a smaller village than the first, yet it ended in disaster. How can this be?"

Pellaidh tugged at his beard, then pointed at the barrier between worlds, a shimmering wall through which the world of the Sons of Mil could be dimly seen.

"Look you," he said. "See how their sun races across the sky? For the folk we just battled, a year and more has passed since our battle. They prepared for our second assault during the year that passed after the first. A single human has so little time, and so treats it as precious, more precious than the Five Talismans are to us. We wile away our long days in games and sport and banquets—all quite worthy, of course—but they fight the earth itself and their own fleet lives just to survive, to reproduce, and to multiply."

"Our magic makes our lives easier. I see." She nodded. "So, how are they to be exterminated?"

"Your pardon, fair lady," said Fenod, who had kept his eye on the veil. "Another, more pressing concern comes to mind."

For there, in the cup between mountains, was gathering a horde of humanity. As each moment passed for the queen and her fellows, an hour and more passed beyond the barrier. And for each of those hours, another throng swelled the ranks of the enemy.

"They trailed us," said Pellaidh, "or I expect there are those who remembered where they were taken for our sport."

"So many," she whispered. Then, aloud, "To arms, all!" She whirled her spear on high. "The enemies are at our door!"

Fenod tugged at Pellaidh's sleeve. "Look," he said. "See how much iron their army carries."

"This will be a mutual slaughter," he said.

"Yes," said Fenod, gazing speculatively at the barrier between worlds. Then he spoke low and urgently to his king. Pellaidh at first shook his head, then stilled and listened, and finally at the end gave a short nod. He patted Fenod on the shoulder and scurried after the queen.

"Milady!" King Pellaidh said without his usual decorousness. "We stand no chance against this horde of humanity. And their numbers only swell, while ours are diminished and threatened with extinction. They are ready to drive us into the Western Sea."

Several buccas and leprechauns muttered their agreement with the brownie king, while others vilified Pellaidh. Aelfric was the first to raise his voice above the chatter.

"We have fought to defend our place here for eons past, but never before a foe that would not accept honorable defeat. These Children of Mil breed like the mayflies they resemble in the briefness of their lives. Without the time to learn honor, they bring no glory in their defeat, yet know no limit in their aggressions."

"True enough," shouted Kheelan from beside him.

"Do we cry done after one lost battle?" asked the queen. "This is unlike the proud Tuatha Dé by whose side I fought 'gainst gods and giants."

"Look at them," said Pellaidh, gesturing at the gathering multitude of humans. "They howl for our blood, as we thirsted for theirs. Even were each of us to slay a dozen of theirs, they'd still carry the day. They've learned the potency of iron. If we meet them, we will all surely die."

As they watched, scouts from the human side approached the divide between lands, carefully feeling before them with staves. When one felt the different quality of the bridge, he called to his fellows. A moment later an elvish arrow took the man's life, but it was too late. Horns sounded, and a column of the enemy formed, ready to advance on the bridge. All this had taken but seconds from the fay's perspective.

"Soon 'twill be too late," said Pellaidh.

"We should leave them to their accursed fields of slaughter and have no more truck with them," Hefeydd added. "We have lands aplenty. Let us retire to Tir Tairngir and curse these humans to never enter the Plain of Happiness."

"Enough," said Medbh. Her quiet voice cut through the clamor. "Let us consult Frige." That silenced the throng and they waited for the goddess to have her final say.

When she appeared, Frige's dour countenance captured the attention of everyone present.

"I hear the lamentations of the dead," she said. "And I feel the grief of the living." She turned a slow circle, catching every eye. Then she nodded.

In her right hand appeared an arrow, now in her left, a bow. The goddess raised her bow, set arrow to string, and loosed. The arrow became a shaft of light, then lightning. When it struck the bridge, a blast of sound swept across the lands, both human and fay, and when it passed, the midspan of the way between worlds was no more. Frige led her subjects on their march away from the portal and the human lands.

Long and long in vain did the humans seek to cross the bridge, to carry their enmity to the Tuatha Dé. Years passed, and decades and centuries, and the fay faded into myth and memory.

~ * ~

A fairy moon rose and set, waned to a sliver and waxed rotund again and the immortal Children of Danu celebrated in their various ways. Pellaidh approached his old retainer where he sat on the edge of Tir Nan Og, staring across to the far shore of the Western Sea, at the world left behind.

"Do you yearn for another place, old friend?" the brownie king asked.

"Nay. This is the land we are best suited for. Nor have I any hankering after times that went before. But I indulge myself by recalling the strange, short-lived folk we abandoned, and wondering how they have fared all these days."

Pellaidh saw right through the elderly elf. He chuckled. "You wonder if they still set out their saucers of milk." Fenod made a show of being shocked at his laird's suggestion. After the hardship they had caused, no sidhe had countenanced having any dealings with the Children of Mil.

"I have thought the same myself," the king confessed. "Let us walk their lands."

The mystic bridge was in ruins, but little enough trouble for agile small folk who after all didn't mind getting wet. Soon they were wandering fields and roads worked by mortal hands. Avoiding contact with humans and marveling at the quiet of a night without spritesong, they came to a small group of cottages and watched as the candles in the windows were blown out one by one.

"I will miss these lands," the King Pellaidh admitted, more to himself than his companion.

"Aye," said Fenod, "'Tis as honorable an end as could be wished. These Children of Mil won fair, but yet they are a sad lot. Unfortunate breed, they toil through their fleeting day while we frolic and sport through ours."

A door opened at the nearby steading, drawing Fenod's attention, then a few moments later closed.

"An offering," he said.

Pellaidh smiled. "Go ahead."

Arriving at the hut, Fenod took off his cap to dip up a small amount. He sipped. Thinking to cheer his majesty, Fenod carried a capful back. Together, share and share, they finished it off.

"I wonder sometimes why they do this," said Fenod.

"Who can divine the ways of humans?" Pellaidh pulled at his beard.

Fenod shrugged, licked his lips and crossed the yard for another hatful. As he noticed a hated iron blade dug deep into a section of tree trunk, he cursed the humans and their dreaded metal. Scattered pieces of trees were more evidence of their perfidy.

He noticed a thin trail of smoke rising over the roof and crept to the window, still thinking of revenge. In the middle of the room, a tiny flame sputtered in a smoky pile of tree segments. Sympathy for the humans's miserable existence washed over him when he saw the puny fire.

As he crossed the yard again, Fenod waved his hand and the wood split into smaller chunks. Then he stopped to draw himself a last cap of milk.

"Our lot is nae so bad," he told his laird.

"It could be far worse." King Pellaidh took another draught.

"We could be humans."

~ * ~ * ~

Manny Frishberg has been making up stories since he first stared out a window. He spent the first half of his life learning how to write them and the second half learning what to write about, He is now spending the third half of his life making up stories, just like when he was eight years old. When he is not doing that, he edits books for small presses and indie authors. His debut novel, "City of Emeralds," a 20th century fantasy-mystery, is due out from 25 and Y books in 2024.

~ * ~ * ~

Edd Vick is a graduate of the Clarion SF Writing Workshop. His stories have appeared in magazines including *Asimovs, Baen's Universe,* and *Analog,* and anthologies including *First Contact Cafe, Fundamentally Challenged,* and *Northwest Passages.* By day a bookseller, he lives in Seattle with SF novelist Amy Thomson (also five chickens, a cat, and a dog).

The Last Son of Auberon

Ben Stewart

Arcadia, in the fifteenth year of the Age of The Dragonfly or 1875, as humans reckon it.

It may seem strange that a race as wise and ancient as the Fay were so oblivious to their oncoming destruction, but the sad truth is that even magical creatures can be doomed by their flaws. The shining lords and ladies who ruled over the magical realm of Arcadia —the most famous of the worlds that sat alongside the main facet of reality, which is occupied by humans—were often prone to arrogance and pride, and likely thought it impossible that anything could threaten their eternal existence. The slow but inexorable pace of the danger also served to disguise it. The seeds of Arcadia's destruction had been sown thousands of years in the past and came to fruition very slowly at first.

Only Lord Auberon, master of the Summer Court, was not ignorant of the growing threat. He had known ever since that day in distant antiquity when primitive humans first discovered the power of fire, and their ascent to the pinnacle of technological advancement began, that Arcadia was doomed. For when technology flourishes, there is progressively less and less room within the confines of existence for magic and wonder.

In the last days before the fall, Lord Auberon had given up his fruitless efforts to convince his fellow lords and ladies of the oncoming danger. Instead he focused on doing what he could to save that which was most precious to him. Toward the conclusion of this task, Auberon could be found chanting softly over an enchanted chestnut shell taken from the great Forest of Tuatha, adding layers of protective wards to the spiky pod by tracing delicate patterns into its surface with a wand fashioned from the roots of a beech sapling. Behind him stood his wife and only ally amongst the courts of the fay, the Lady Morgyanna. Morgyanna listened to her husband's incantation whilst cradling a tiny bundle of blankets to her chest. That bundle contained the one thing in Arcadia she held most dear—her infant son, Robyn. He was her thirteenth and last living child.

She gazed lovingly at the child sleeping in her arms. The baby clutched a lock of her long golden hair in one pudgy fist and slumbered in perfect serenity, utterly unaware of the oncoming danger that would destroy the world that he had not even yet begun to experience. When Auberon's chanting came to a halt, Morgyanna could not bring herself to lift her eyes away from her beloved son.

"It is done already?" she asked, fighting to keep her voice from breaking. Auberon nodded.

"It is time, my love," he said, as gently as he could. He reached out to take his son from his wife's arms, but Morgyanna did not hand the child over.

"Morgyanna… It is the only way."

Still Morgyanna did not look up. Auberon placed an arm around her slender shoulders and held both his wife and son close to his chest.

"Think of our lost sons," he said. "Perivale, slain by the foul wyrm Lloygor. Eremar and Tristane, fallen at the Battle of Four Lakes, and so many others. Twelve children that we have outlived. Their loss weighs heavy on my soul, Morgyanna. If I can save our last child then I must do so, no matter what it takes."

"I have never doubted you before, Auberon, but when I face separation from my last child, I must ask again. You are certain that Arcadia will fall?"

Auberon sighed. He lifted Robyn from Morgyanna's arms, carefully freeing the tress of hair the infant held for comfort.

"The other courts of the fay may chose to ignore me, but I have no doubts. I have read the signs and portents and seen the warnings in the stars. I have spoken to the animals that are loyal to our court. I, unlike the rest of our kin, still visit the mortal realm on occasion. They do not even understand why they no longer feel the need to walk amongst the mortals, but I have felt the oppressive aura of tedium and logic that saturates that plane. And now that aura reaches even bright Arcadia."

Morgyanna's tears began to flow freely as Auberon carried Robyn toward the chestnut shell.

"But why must he be sent to the very realm that will destroy our home?" she sobbed. "Why must he endure its insidious stench of reason and logic?"

"It is the only option. The human world is the only one I am certain I can guide the pod to before the end comes. I have now gifted unto him the entirety of my strength and magical skill, which I pray will be enough for him to survive in such a hostile realm. I cannot save Arcadia, Morgyanna—my arts are not powerful enough. But I believe I can protect one being from the incoming tide of staleness and rationality that seeps from the human minds that will surround him."

Auberon gently placed his sleeping son into the awaiting shell. The pod already contained other items that the lord of the Summer Court had selected to teach the child the heritage of a people he would never know—books containing the wisdom and the history of the realm of the fay, small portraits of a family the child would never know, and a lengthy letter that tried to explain the circumstances that had led to this tragic situation. But most importantly of all, Auberon included his son's birthright—the Armor of the Summer Lord. This exquisite suit of golden plate had been crafted by the greatest artisan in the long history of Arcadia, and now waited, bound in spider-silk, for the day Robyn was old enough to wear it into battle.

Holding each other close, Auberon and Morgyanna wept together as the pod closed its two halves together and then slowly faded from sight with a twinkling of tiny golden stars, traveling onward to the location in the realm of humanity that Auberon had thought best suited to be Robyn's new home. Praying to all of the Gods of the Arcadian pantheon that their son would be safe, the lord and lady of the Summer Court waited for the end to come.

Mere hours later, the tide of banality crushed the last vestiges of Arcadia's magical defenses, and the realm of the Shining Folk was lost forever. This terrible event was felt by every living being in the universe to some degree, if only as a subconscious tremor of fear or a nightmare-wracked sleep. Shock-waves rippled throughout space and time and were even felt in the distant past and far future. The fay vanished from existence and their magic was extinguished from the universe—all except for one last beacon of light that materialized in a dense pine forest, selected by Lord Auberon for its resemblance to the Forest of Tuatha.

In a sun-dappled glade surrounded by mighty oaks, Robyn safely snoozed in the pod fashioned by his father. The story of Arcadia had reached its catastrophic conclusion, but the Last Son of Auberon had survived—and the story of his life was still to be written.

Southwood City, 1938

Karen Appleby was momentarily dazzled when the rough cloth bag was yanked off her head. Her eyes were unaccustomed to light after spending God only knew how long in darkness. She was also still woozy from the chloroform that had been used in her abduction, and her wrists and ankles hurt terribly where they were tied painfully tight to the chair in which she was sat. All in all, this evening had not gone the way she had planned.

Karen had just reached the end one of the strangest and most stressful weeks of her life. She had only escaped alive thanks to the intervention of a somewhat unusual old friend of hers. After this nightmarish week, Karen had intended to try and unwind by spending the evening representing the company she and her father owned, Appleby Industrial and Chemical, at a charity ball held by the Mayor's office. She didn't normally enjoy such swanky affairs, being more comfortable in a lab coat than the expensive floor-length red silk evening gown she currently wore. But after having to deal with industrial espionage, sabotage and the F. B. I., Karen had thought she'd earned a spot of rest and relaxation. She'd even been willing to put up with the tedious advances of the lecherous, overweight businessmen that were a common feature of such events. Such men only saw her as a twenty-something slim, attractive, brunette rather than a Harvard-educated research scientist who was possibly the best chemical engineer in America, but she'd thought an evening of clumsy pick-up lines would be easier to endure than another round of questions from interchangeable, humorless G-men.

Unfortunately any chance of a pleasant evening had gone out the window when she'd hailed a cab on her way to the party, only to find a bull-necked goon of a man waiting for her in the back seat when she'd jumped in. The last thing she could remember was the fake cab speeding away while the thug jammed the chemical-soaked rag into her face. Then nothing but deceptively peaceful darkness, until she'd woken up in her current predicament.

Slowly, Karen's eyes became accustomed to the light and she could see she was sat in the middle of a warehouse of some kind. Most likely at Southwood City's run-down riverside dock district, she reckoned. The place looked like it hadn't been in regular use for quite a while, with a only a few sorry-looking packing crates scattered around its cavernous interior. She ignored the crates however, being more interested in the five men who stood before her. She recognized one of them as the man who had chloroformed her—a coarsely-featured, unshaven brute of a man in oil-stained denims and heavy work boots whose kind was a dime a dozen in this neighborhood. Three of the other men were cut from the same cloth, more cheap hired muscle.

It was the fifth man who held Karen's attention. She had grown to hate this man more than any other in the last seven days, and she had guessed he was behind her kidnapping as soon as she'd had a moment to consider it. The man was much smaller than his ape-like companions, and much better dressed. He was a slim fellow of about fifty, possessed of refined, angular features and a long, delicate fingers. He was completely bald and hid his eyes behind glasses with smoked lenses, which gave him a sinister air. His expensive, tailored gray suit and overcoat were immaculately clean, and his shoes buffed to a mirror shine. This made him look quite out of place in the company of dockside roughs in a derelict warehouse. Karen's eyes locked onto the man as soon as she saw him. He seemed to find the expression of hatred written plainly on her face to be quite amusing, and met it with a cruel grin.

"Ah, Miss Appleby." His educated, and very convincing, New England accent was thick with theatrical joviality. "So glad you could join us this evening. May I say you do look very pretty tonight, my dear. You should wear your hair down more often, it really does suit you."

"Doctor Oliver Cross," spat Karen with genuine venom. "Or should I call you by your real name, Doctor Otto von Koloss? Do these meatheads know they're working for a Nazi stooge?"

Koloss laughed heartily.

"My dear Miss Appleby. I see that the F.B.I. was kind enough to furnish you with my correct name. That will save me introducing myself again, at least. And I'm afraid these good fellows know fine well what I am. They are far more interested in my money than my politics, and I do rather have a lot money to play with."

Karen yanked futilely at her bounds once more.

"I thought you'd be back in Germany by now, Koloss," she said. "Trying to explain to your fruit-and-nutjob tyrant of a boss that you'd failed to get your hands on our high-energy fuel formula."

"I shall be returning to the Fatherland presently, Miss Appleby. I still have a few loose ends to attend to in your U.S.A., you see. Though it is a shame I could not secure your formula, as its chemical composition did include some concepts that were really quite interesting. Impressive work on your part, especially when one considers your inferior gender."

Karen wrenched at her bonds with a renewed fury after that remark.

"You untie these damned ropes and I'll show you how inferior my gender is! I'll kick you in the clams so hard they'll end up getting stuck in your damn Nazi throat!"

Koloss roared in laughter, slapping his thigh in his mirth.

"Oh, most amusing Miss Appleby! Most amusing indeed! You always were a feisty one! But I feel I should point out that I have four men stationed inside this warehouse and a further five outside. I fear you might struggle to deal with all of us in your 'clam kicking' plan."

"Well that doesn't matter, does it, you chrome-dome, fifth-column fascist. *He'll* find me. He can always find his friends when we're in trouble."

"You are, of course, correct. You always were a smart one, Miss Appleby. It's such a shame that you reacted so poorly when you discovered the real reason I came to work for A.I.C. Had you been more amenable to my plans, you could have made a most capable assistant."

Koloss reached into his suit jacket pocket, and Karen gulped as he took out a surgeon's scalpel. Its wickedly sharp blade glinted in the cold glare of the electric lights.

"As you say, Miss Appleby, *he* always finds his friends and comes to their rescue when they are in trouble. Unfortunately, I cannot wait all night for this inevitable confrontation. We may have to increase the amount of trouble you are in to hurry him along."

Koloss tested the point of the scalpel with the tip of a finger. Finding it to be to his satisfaction, he started toward Karen with a sick grin plastered across his face.

"Take not one more step toward her, villain! Your reckoning has come!" The stentorian but melodic voice rang out from somewhere in the dark roof space of the warehouse, and all eyes instantly snapped upward.

The man who had called out was visible even in the shadowy recesses of the roof, for he seemed to glow with an inner luminescence that made it difficult to see him in detail, but everyone present knew exactly what the newcomer looked like. They knew fine well he was clad from neck to foot in master-crafted, close-fitting golden armor decorated with intricate scroll-work patterns. They could all picture the delicately handsome features covered only by a small bandit-style mask woven from silver thread that sat across his high cheekbones, and the mane of jet-black hair tumbling freely about his shoulders. And they, along with every other citizen of that fair city, would have recognized the image of an eagle with its wings spread etched onto the armor's breastplate. But rather than recognizing the device as the coat of arms of the Summer Court of the Fay, they would refer to the resplendent eagle as the symbol of Captain Arcadian, the Golden Guardian of Southwood City. The 'Golden Guardian' was but one of the usually alliterative affectionate epithets coined by the media to describe the city's favorite citizen, such was the high regard in which he was held. The champion of justice and the scourge of the criminal class, the ever-youthful Captain Arcadian had been the protector of the good citizens of Southwood City for almost thirty years. He had foiled bank robberies, thwarted kidnappers, broken gangs and most recently played a key role in uncovering the machinations of a certain Nazi spy. The Sparkling Sentinel struck fear into the hearts of criminals everywhere, including Koloss's toughs, who all retreated a few paces at the sight of him—despite the fact he was only six inches tall.

"Am I pleased to see you, Captain!" called out Karen. "Dr. Sauerkraut here was starting to get a little bit too frisky for my liking!"

"Fear not, fair Karen," replied the Pixie Protector. "This base fiend has troubled you and evaded his deserved fate for the final time. Tonight, this matter shall be finally settled."

Captain Arcadian hopped lightly from his lofty perch. Instantly his shimmering, dragonfly-like wings snapped into action, carrying him gently downward. As he descended, he gestured toward Koloss and his men with one gleaming gauntlet-covered hand.

"Come now, you ill-favored miscreants, let battle be joined!"

"You heard Mr. Tinker Bell, boys!" cackled Koloss. "Don't keep him waiting!"

Captain Arcadian halted his descent, hovering about six feet above the filthy warehouse floor as the five goons formed a rough semi-circle around him. They all knew full well just what the Impossible Imp was capable of, and none were too keen to make the first move. After a few seconds of this tense face-off, one man found his courage and lunged forward with a wild haymaker of a punch.

With lightning-quick reflexes, Captain Arcadian darted out of the path of his clumsy attack. The man's fist instead thudded into the face of one of his allies who had been approaching from the other side, sending the unlucky fellow sprawling with a broken nose. Before the puncher could react, Captain Arcadian flew in front of his face and simply tapped him gently on the forehead. Instantly the ruffian collapsed to the floor where he began snoring loudly, trapped in a magically induced slumber. Two more men dived into the fray, but the Shining Sprite clapped his golden gauntlets together and for a split second the halo of radiance about him flared into a scintillating flash of light that caused both men to cry out and turn away, covering their dazzled eyes. As the pair stumbled about blindly, one tripped over his sleeping crony and hit the ground with a meaty thud, while another lurched face-first into a packing crate, then slumped to the floor. Both stayed down.

The last man standing had hung back during the first moments of the skirmish and now took another few steps back. After seeing three of his fellow goons dealt with in mere seconds, he was ,even less keen to tangle with the Enchanted Avenger. Karen recognized this last man as the one who had accosted her in the back of the dummy cab.

"Hey Captain!" she shouted, "give that mook something special! He's the creep that chloroformed me!"

"It shall be as the lady wishes," replied Captain Arcadian, bowing respectfully to Karen in mid-air as the crook recovered his nerve and made a grab for the Winged Wonder. The hero reacted swiftly, reaching into a tiny pouch on his belt and throwing a handful of sparking dust from it straight at his attacker. The handful became a glittering cloud bigger than it had any right to be given the size of the hand that had held it, which engulfed the kidnapper entirely. As the man tried to wipe the fairy dust from his face, the miraculous substance took effect and the bully rose free of gravity's grasp, slowly spinning head over heels as he drifted up into the rafters.

"Nice one, Captain!" yelled Karen in amusement, enjoying the look of shock on the man's ugly face and his howls of terror as he tried desperately to grab hold of a light fitting to control his sudden ascent.

Suddenly the warehouse door burst open and the balance of Koloss's men stormed in, no doubt alerted by the commotion of the fight within.

"So pleased you could make it," said Koloss sarcastically. "'Now why don't you boys try and earn your rather generous paychecks by dealing with this Cottingley reject, eh?"

The five men charged. With a flutter of iridescent wings Captain Arcadian flew to meet them, trailing light like a tiny comet. Clearly the Diminutive Daredevil's patience was wearing thin by this time, as rather than using fay glamours and enchantments to deal with the late arrivals he instead opted for a more direct approach. Flying at a remarkable speed, the Shining Sprite aimed himself squarely at the lead man's nose, hitting it harder than would have seemed possible given his Lilliputian stature. From there, he ricocheted from man to man like a deflecting bullet, striking them in the face, stomach, groin and so on until each had been reduced to a whimpering heap of pain, writhing on the warehouse floor. Once his last foe had been despatched, Captain Arcadian flitted to face Doctor Otto von Koloss, who was now the last man to stand between him and his friend.

"This is your last chance, Koloss," stated Captain Arcadian grimly. "Release Karen and surrender quietly or I shall have to use force, which is actually something I would very much enjoy in this circumstance."

"Hmm, let me see…" Koloss mockingly pretended to mull the question over. "I'm sorry, my little friend, but as nice as being arrested and handed over the F.B.I. sounds, I'm afraid I shall have to decline."

Arcadian nodded. "So be it. This ends now, Koloss."

The Miniature Marvel beat his wings and charged straight toward his final opponent, but the Nazi doctor moved with surprising speed as he grabbed a small bundle from his suit pocket and hurled it toward the onrushing fay. The bundle opened into a net about two feet square, and due to his velocity Captain Arcadian could not avoid it. To Karen's horror, as soon as Arcadian was entangled in the net's strands he tumbled out of the air as if shot by a hidden sniper. As he skidded to a halt on the cold floor his natural glow faded to nothingness, and he lay still.

"What the hell have you done to him?" cried Karen, once more trying to free her hands from the ropes that held them. Koloss laughed in triumph.

"Your 'Golden Guardian' yet lives, Miss Appleby, but my net has successfully nullified all of his fay abilities! I've done my research, you see. I studied so many tomes of myths and legends to find a way to counter his magical abilities, and I discovered the common tales of how cold iron was the fay's great weakness. But this could not just be any iron. Not since Captain Arcadian spends so much of his time in this city of iron and glass, eh?"

Karen could only watch helplessly as Koloss grandstanded before her. From this distance she couldn't even tell if the tiny hero was breathing or not.

"No, normal iron couldn't be the answer," Koloss continued. "Then I read of thunderbolt iron, which was said to be the ideal form of iron for dealing with fay—iron taken from the heart of meteorites, no less. And then I finally discovered the remarkable truth. According to one esoteric scholar's work, the iron at the heart of a meteorite is actually a solidified chunk of the wave of logic that the author predicted would annihilate the Fairy home dimension, scattered through space and time by the force of the land's destruction. It would seem that both his prediction and theory were correct. That net is made of wires forged from thunderbolt iron taken from a meteorite that crashed near Düsseldorf, and it has overcame the hero of Southwood City with ease!"

"You've killed him, you twisted bastard!" Karen fought back tears of rage, and still Koloss continued to taunt her.

"Oh no, Miss Appleby. He will likely recover once the net is removed. He'll be fine, I assure you. Well, for now, at least. My orders are to take him back to Germany, where I shall dissect him in the hope of finding a way to harness and replicate his magical abilities for use by the Fatherland. I'm afraid I was never really interested in your formula—that was just a ruse to draw Arcadian out. Don't worry though, Miss Appleby, you are not entirely superfluous. I'm sure I can find use for an attractive young woman such as your self back in Germany. I'm sure you will make a most enjoyable 'assistant.'"

Maddened by anger, Karen wrenched again and again at her bonds as Koloss continued to gloat over the fallen fairy. She fought until blood ran freely down her wrists but still she refused to quit, despite the futility of her efforts. Then, just as even her steely determination was starting to waver, something brushed past her fingers. Something furry. Karen froze. Something briefly touched her ankle too, and then she felt a series of little tugs at the ropes that held her. Koloss was ignoring her, choosing instead to direct his mockery at the trapped Captain Arcadian. Karen risked a look at was was around her feet and had to choke back a scream of shock. Big, fat, black wharf rats were frantically nibbling at her bonds with their sharp, yellowed incisors. Five or six of them were at her feet and a look behind the chair showed a similar number chewing away at the ropes on her wrists. Beady eyes gleamed, fleshy tails flicked wildly.

They were freeing her! This must somehow be the the work of Captain Arcadian, and so resisted her natural impulse to shoo them away. The murine rescuers worked quickly, and after a only a few seconds Karen was able to work her hands and feet free of the severely gnawed ropes. Koloss still had his back to her, so she stood as quietly as she could manage and hitched up the hem of her evening gown in readiness.

"Paging Doctor Otto von Chump!" she called brightly.

The doctor turned to face her, the smug look of triumph melting from his face as he saw his captive was free. He didn't have a chance to do anything else, however, as Karen made good on her earlier promise and delivered a brutal punt with very tip of her high-heeled shoes squarely into the Nazi scientist's groin. Koloss doubled over, letting out a long, high-pitched gasp of agony, and Karen followed up with a stinging right uppercut that put him on his rear.

With Koloss out of the picture at least temporarily, Karen dashed over to Captain Arcadian. The Pint-sized Paladin was lying so very still, thoroughly entangled in the cold iron net. Karen began to free him from the thin wire strands, unhooking threads where they had snagged on his golden armour and taking great care to protect his fragile wings.

"C'mon, Captain. Just you hang on. I'm going to get you out of this, so help me God…" Karen muttered to herself nervously as she worked, praying that Koloss had been right about the net's effects not being permanent.

After several minutes of diligent work that felt like long hours to Karen, she finally unwound the last strand from where it had caught on one of Arcadian's pauldrons and hurled the evil net as far as she could across the warehouse. Freed from the baleful influence of the cold iron Captain Arcadian's inner glow returned, albeit it very weakly, and he started to stir.

He tried to speak but only managed to faintly croak one word. "Koloss…"

"Don't you worry about that loser, Captain," replied Karen. "I've got him right here—"

Karen looked over her shoulder, but to her dismay the doctor had gone. Only his overcoat remained to mark the spot where he had lain moments earlier. The sudden roar of a car engine from outside, followed by the squealing of tires as the vehicle sped away, told the whole story. Koloss must have hobbled off to his escape vehicle while Karen had been engrossed in rescuing Arcadian. She swore softly under her breath, but decided that then and there she had more important things to worry about.

"Sorry, Captain, but Koloss has cheesed it again," she said as she tenderly picked up the enervated warrior, holding him close. "But don't fret about that, he'll be back for another round soon enough. Right now, we just need to get you home."

~ * ~

The next day was a remarkably pleasant one, despite the coming of autumn. Clear skies and an unseasonably warm sun made Kent Park, Southwood City's largest green space, a popular destination for the residents. Kent Park was all that remained of a much older area of wilderness which had been swallowed up by the city's rapid expansion since its founding just before the turn of the century. Only one copse remained of the ancient trees that had once covered this landscape. Despite the wooded vale's central location and the fact the park was so busy on this fine day, few people went near the venerable oaks. For some reason, most visitors to the park simply never seemed to notice the small forest. This was due to a fay glamour woven over the area by Captain Arcadian to protect the remains of the wood his parents had intended to be his new home all those years ago. Residents of Southwood City simply ignored the trees as if they were not there. Only those the Golden Guardian wished to meet could find their way into the glade's heart, where he lived still.

Karen sat on the mossy ground, leaning against one of the mighty oaks of Arcadian's sanctuary. She still wore the fine evening gown she had intended to show off at the previous night's ball, but had supplemented it with Koloss's fine woollen overcoat to protect against the chill. She had stayed with Arcadian all night to ensure that he was suffering no lasting effects from Koloss's cold iron trap, and it seemed he was now fully recovered. The Gleaming Gladiator was perched on a branch high above the glade. He had removed his golden armor and mask, and now wore a shimmering robe of shifting reds and brown that mirrored the hues of the autumnal leaves around him. At that moment he was not Captain Arcadian, hero of Southwood City, but simply Robyn, the Last Son of Auberon and sole surviving scion of Arcadia. Opening his wings, Robyn flitted down to a lower branch a few feet from Karen.

"I must thank you once more for returning me here, Karen. After a few hours spent in even this small fragment of nature's splendor I am feeling much more like myself."

Karen smiled. "Don't mention it, Robbie. Given the number of times you've saved my skin it's about time I returned the favor. But you played your part too, I think. I take it those rats were your doing?"

"Quite so. My father was the lord of Arcadia's Summer Court, and so was blessed with powers over both plants and animals. Amongst the many gifts my parents bestowed upon me is a vestige of that power. My father summoned foxes or eagles to act as his steeds in battle, or swift hares to carry messages to his compatriots. There are, of course, fewer creatures to call upon in a city such as this, but while the humble rat may appear to be a baser beast he can still be staunch ally."

A few moments passed in silence, as the two friends listened to to chirp of birds and the rustle of the breeze in the treetops. Eventually Karen voiced aloud the topic that she knew Robyn was silently pondering.

"So what about Koloss?"

"I should hunt him, of course, but I fear that ultimately it will be a futile gesture."

"What do you mean? I know he got the drop on you with that hideous net, but you'll be ready for that trick next time, yeah?"

"It is not Koloss I fear, Karen. He is but one head of a terrible hydra that possesses a million and more terrible, slavering maws. Even with him captured, his fellows and their vile leader will continue their nefarious schemes. There is nothing I can do to stop the war that I can feel coming. War like mankind has never known."

Robyn stared wistfully at a pair of starlings that had alighted on a branch opposite. "I told you what I know about the death of my people, haven't I?"

Karen nodded solemnly.

"Destroyed by the indifference of mankind. Destroyed by the world of technology that washed over the world of magic. But the hatred and anger of mankind played it's part too. There is no place for a realm as beautiful as Arcadia was in world of naked intolerance and slaughter, and that is exactly what approaches. My parents did their utmost to shield me against the horrors of this realm, but the atmosphere of evil created by the myriad horrors of the so-called Great War nearly killed me twenty years ago. My foes may have discovered the power of thunderbolt iron, and it is a grim reminder of what befell my forefathers, but I think ultimately they will not need it to slay me. I fear even the protections my parents gifted me will not withstand the atrocities I sense are coming."

Robyn's melancholy words prompted more silence. Once more it was Karen who chose to break it.

"So what are you going to do? Sit here and wait to be crushed under an avalanche of the garbage of war? Or are you going to fight it?"

Robyn laughed, and flashed Karen a broad smile.

"Of course you are correct. You always did have a way of breaking problems down to a simple solution. I suppose it is what makes you so skilled at your science. If my end must come, then I should meet it like a true Son of Auberon, fighting to my last breath.

And before that time comes, I have a score to settle. My armor beckons, Karen. Doctor Otto von Koloss has enjoyed a night of freedom that he did not deserve, and I do not intend to allow him another."

Robyn beat his wings and zipped back into the upper reaches of the tree, towards a hollow that served as his home.

Karen called after him. "Wait! There's one more thing!"

Hovering in mid-air, Robyn turned back to his friend.

"If what you say is true, if this coming war will be the end of you… What then?"

Robyn considered the question carefully.

"If that should come to pass, then the last remnant of Arcadia will be gone from reality. But if I have reminded the world in some small way of that blessed domain by my actions, then I shall be satisfied. Remember me, Karen. Remember Captain Arcadian and the realms of the fay in the new stories and myths I have tried to create. Hopefully I can remind humanity that they need not completely disregard magic and wonder."

With that, Robyn disappeared into the trunk of the tree to retrieve the trappings of his valiant alter-ego. Southwood City's Golden Guardian would fly again that day, and a villain who had evaded justice for too long would surely meet his destiny.

~ * ~ * ~

A resident of the dark and frozen reaches of Northern England, **Ben Stewart** is an aspiring writer who cites the pulp greats like Howard, Lovecraft, Wagner and Burroughs as his main influences. He is an inveterate geek with a love of Japanese Kaiju movies, super-hero comics and miniature wargaming, but despite this he's somehow married with three kids. Ben has managed to get a handful of his short stories published in various anthologies though his ultimate goal of actually completing a novel-length work still eludes him.

INKED OUT

Brandy T. Wilson

It was Liz's first day at her new job. A real job, where she was going to blow them away with her got-her-shit-togetherness, her age-appropriateness. But she had to get there first, in one piece, and dressed in decent clothes. Clothes that covered... Well, that covered up her entire twenties.

"What the hell is 'casually corporate,' anyway?" she asked herself as she stumbled over a pile of books and a mound of shoes on her way to the closet. She'd intended to sort and organize the piles before the start of her new job, but she couldn't ever seem to get up early enough. She kicked through the shoes and picked up one stack of books, placing it neatly on top of a box of un-built shelves.

"That's a step," she said, and opened her closet door.

Her old boss and coworkers had thrown her a going-away party the previous week at the bar where Liz had worked for the last four years. It had been fun, but she'd woken up with a hangover so bad that she couldn't even go to brunch the next day to top it off.

She had overstayed her welcome in that scene. She was paranoid that she looked like an overgrown kid, or worse, like the sad old cougar at the end of the bar. Either way, unattractive. When she thought about it all, it left a bad taste in her mouth. She'd had trouble sleeping ever since.

She rubbed her sleep-filled eyes and opened the closet door. Her wardrobe was staggeringly full of short skirts and slinky tops, even though she had managed to organize and clean it out the previous week. She thought she'd left one longer skirt in there. Even if it were out of fashion, she'd wear it anyway. She had blazers she could wear over any number of slinky tops, if she could just find that skirt.

As a door girl/go-go dancer in college, it wasn't so much what she wore as how little it covered, but now, years after graduation, it was getting harder to pull off this look, even at the bar. Liz thumbed through the clothes all the way to the back of the closet, but she still couldn't find the long skirt. When she saw the time, a prick of panic struck her stomach. She grabbed every skirt she owned and tossed it, still halfway clinging to its hanger, toward the bed. Then she yanked out a few old blouses she hadn't seen since her freshman year and attempted to match them up. The blue skirt she'd worn to her first college party was a little tight and revealing, but it passed inspection next to her longest black mini-skirt, which came to just above the knee. With a jacket, she was convinced the outfit would pass.

She draped the ensemble over the bedpost and stumbled over the new pile of clothes toward the bathroom. She jerked her nightgown over her head and turned on the shower. The water was warm against her sensitive skin, and it calmed her.

"I'll never smell like a brewery again," she thought.

Liz turned off the shower and sat down to shave her legs. With only one stroke, bright blues and greens began to peek through the shaving cream. Liz sank into the tub and dropped the razor. Until that moment, she had forgotten the free tattoo she'd gotten for 'knowing the right people' —that is, people who hung out with tattoo artists. Since her early twenties, the larger-than-she-intended flower and fairy had become such a part of her leg that she barely noticed it anymore.

At first, she had hated the distorted thing with its strange wings that looked more like feathers, hair that looked like a toddler had drawn it, and pointed anorexic features. Still, it had grown on her. The missing leg and nippled breasts weren't as noticeable now that it had faded a bit, and the ivy she'd added to it downplayed the edgy, bright blue clouds that outlined the scene. But now, as Liz picked up the razor again, all these features seemed to flood back into her skin, brighter and bolder than ever. Even the unrecognizable blob that was supposed to be a flower was more pronounced and less like a backdrop.

"I can't wear a skirt. I don't have any hose dark enough to cover this hideous thing!" She scrambled out of the tub, dried herself haphazardly, and went dripping back to the closet, now half-empty and with few pants in sight. She'd already returned her friend Kris's pantsuit that she'd worn for the interview. "Those would be too dressy anyway."

Liz tore the remaining clothes from the front of the closet and found her 'inspiration pants,' the pair she refused to throw out because, in her mind, they reminded her how small she once was and still could be if she tried hard enough. Liz wasn't so much over-weight as short and muscular, with a torso and thighs that wouldn't fit into regularly cut parts, so she rarely wore them. She pulled on the snug black pants, forcing them over her hips, but no matter how hard she tugged, she couldn't button them. She pulled on the shirt and jacket anyway, and saw the unbuttoned pants and the tightness in the legs and rear were just hidden by the tail end of the jacket. The pants were a bit too short, but they did their job of covering the tattoo. In her rush to leave, she put on a pair of dress shoes and forced herself to walk away from the mirror unimpressed.

Liz arrived at her new job punctually, but not as early as she had planned. She was winded when she reached her boss's office.

"Good morning, Liz. Come on in." Sandra stood to walk around her desk, reaching out to shake Liz's hand. She was dressed in a snug navy cosmopolitan suit with wonderfully hip, wedged heels and bare legs.

"I think I'd rather go by Elizabeth now, if you don't mind," Liz said.

"Sure! Elizabeth is a beautiful name. That's just fine," Sandra said. "Well, Elizabeth, since you'll be my assistant, I'd like you to come with me to a meeting this morning. This client is planning a shareholders convention, and I am trying to convince him that fresh oysters are almost impossible to get at this time of year. I just got off the phone with a frantic chef who doesn't want her reputation ruined by bad seafood." Sandra gave Elizabeth a legal pad and pen, and led her out of the office to the conference room. "I think he will want a full bar, which is fine, but we will need to round up some bartenders. The caterers don't supply them."

Elizabeth nodded, but had the strangest sensation while she walked. She felt a burst of cool air at her ankle, going up her pants leg. She reached down to smooth the cuff, and it was higher, snagged, like it was lifted just above her tattoo. She almost lost her footing, imagining the tattooed fairy was veering its ugly little head from under her already-too-short pants leg as it rose a little with each step. She caught the eyes of the two secretaries, who appeared to be glaring at her leg. She sped up to a brisk shuffle beside Sandra's long strides. Once in the conference room, she stood with the tattoo facing away from Sandra and tried not to appear rigid as she leaned across the table to shake their client's hand.

When they had seated themselves, she pulled her chair as close to the table as she could, and crossed her ankles with her right foot awkwardly leaning out. By this time she was in a sweat, and the bold colors of the fairy flashed across her sight with each blink.

Their client, Mr. Wallace, was a large man, well dressed in a dark suit and conservative, pale yellow tie. His sharp features changed from greeting to a stern look of business as Sandra began her spiel.

"Oysters are good, especially when shipped in the -ber months —September, October, November, and December. I'm afraid they aren't a good idea in May." When Sandra offered other suggestions, he leaned back and folded his arms across his chest, resting his eyes directly on Elizabeth.

"And how do you feel about oysters, Elizabeth?" His question had an oddly rhetorical tone.

"I don't care for seafood myself, sir," Elizabeth blurted through her nerves. "The chance of having oysters that are anything less than fresh or in season makes my stomach turn."

Sandra gave a tense laugh and Mr. Wallace pushed back from the table to lean forward with his hands on his knees.

"Well, since you put it that way," he laughed, "I guess rotten seafood wouldn't make a good impression on the shareholders."

They all laughed, and Sandra continued with a sigh of relief. Elizabeth pushed back a little from the table herself. While she listened, she leaned against the back of the chair, hoping her zipper would slip just a bit to release the tension on her tight pants.

"Do you want a full bar, or just wine and beer?" Sandra asked. "Both will need bartenders."

Elizabeth leaned forward again, but stopped herself when she was about to speak up. She knew a dozen bartenders who would jump at the chance to work an event like this one. She herself could sling drinks if need be, but she was terrified that the person she was then would get her fired from this job. She'd known how to have a good time when she was working at the bar. She was loud and crass, dancing seductively and singing along with whatever song was on as she welcomed customers.

"I think the shareholders will be expecting a full bar, don't you? Do you have someone to bartend? We'd probably need a pretty big setup, don't you think?"

Sandra glanced over at Elizabeth, as if prodding her to offer a suggestion. Elizabeth ducked her head and took notes. She wanted a clean break from that life. She still cringed when she thought of her last weekend at the bar, relieved she couldn't fully remember what she'd said and done. None of that mattered at the bar, but now… She didn't want any part of that life to touch her new life. Without looking up, she scribbled down the numbers the client gave for attendance and the number of bar setups they'd need.

Just as she was finishing the notes, she felt that cold sensation at her ankle again, like it was exposed. She leaned over to get a look at her leg, while trying to seem attentive to the conversation. In her quick glance, she saw a splotch of green from the tattoo. She tugged at the hem of her pants, but with her legs crossed they wouldn't stay down. Sandra and the client stopped talking and looked at her for just a beat, but long enough. She stopped fidgeting and tried to casually hold her ankle with both hands. Just as Sandra and Mr. Wallace rose from their seats, Elizabeth felt a little prick on her hand.

"Ouch!" She pulled her hand back. There was a tiny speck of blood right in the center, as if someone had pressed a needle into her palm. Elizabeth glanced down at her ankle again, and there appeared to be something moving under her pants leg.

"Are you okay?" Sandra asked.

Elizabeth stammered, "Oh, yeah, I'm… I'm fine. There must be a pin in the hem of my pants or something."

Sandra smiled and they both shook hands with the client. When he was gone, she took Elizabeth to her new office. After a tour of all the equipment, Sandra gave Elizabeth a list of clients to call and explained each little note of instructions by the names. Once settled and finally alone, Elizabeth could not wait to take a peek at the tattoo. She slowly lifted up her pants leg. As the tattoo became visible, she was so startled she accidentally kicked over the trash can by her feet trying to jerk away from her own ankle. The fairy's wand looked different, as if it had moved, but then she couldn't remember what it had looked like before. It stood erect in the fairy's hand, when she could swear it had pointed downward, toward her foot. The yellow glow at the end seemed brighter than ever, and Elizabeth could have sworn the fairy found some way to grin at her inspection.

"Everything all right in there? You need some help?" the secretary asked as she opened the door.

Elizabeth scrambled to pick up the trash can. "Just a little clumsy today, I guess. I've got it, thanks," she laughed.

The rest of the day went by quickly and a bit more smoothly. She was able to work alone in her office, and there were no more tattoo alarms. That evening, Elizabeth sat down with the phone book and called every number that advertised laser tattoo removal. The cost was always about the same—too much, unless she got another credit card to max out, which she wasn't willing to do. Exasperated, she went out and bought dark tights, knee socks, and three pairs of dress pants on the way to see her best friend, Kris.

"I will cover it up better from now on," she said. "I haven't had enough sleep, and I've been so anxious. Now that this first day is over, I think I'll be fine."

"Why don't you just let your tattoo show?" Kris asked. "Event planning isn't exactly a conservative or prudish job."

"The job may not be, but some of the clients are. Besides, I don't care how fun or laid back the people I work with are, they are still quite a bit older and more established. They probably associate tattoos with bikers or prison. And it's so ugly, Kris! It looks like a blob from a distance, and it's horribly drawn up close."

"If you ask me, you're just being silly and paranoid, Liz. But that's what you get for taking a free tattoo from a guy named Cyclops."

"What did I know? I was only nineteen, and I didn't have friends like you around to set me straight."

Kris nodded and went to the refrigerator. She came back to the table with a bottle of wine and two glasses, but Elizabeth refused a glass.

"Oh, and I'm using my full name now, too."

"Excuse me, Elizabeth the corporate queen, formerly known as Liz the bar girl!" Kris laughed.

"You don't have to make it sound so corny. I'm serious about this job—the whole bit. You should see my bedroom. I've got everything all ready to get organized. I'm finally going to be a grown-up. A successful woman, not some fly-by-the-seat-of-my-pants gal from the bar who stumbled home too late every night after too much wine."

"Give me a break. First of all, you've always been a success. You were a straight-A student, but organized?" Kris shook her head. "Tell me, what does your closet that you wasted an entire weekend 'organizing' look like now?"

Elizabeth looked away sheepishly.

"That's what I thought. Don't worry about the tattoo. It's not that bad, and it's a part of you."

Elizabeth hugged Kris and thanked her before leaving. Intent on her new image, she still had no intention of showing her tattoo in public again. She would prove herself if it killed her.

"I didn't bust my ass in school for what turned out to be five and a half years for nothing," she said, pointing defiantly at her tattoo while she drove, "and you are not going to screw this up for me!"

That night, she dreamed she had forgotten to wear tights under her skirt, leaving the tattoo exposed for all to see. She was too terrified in the dream to enter her boss's office. In the morning, it took her an hour to find the tights she'd just bought at the store. Apparently, she'd left them by the front door, still in the shopping bag. When she opened the bag, she found that one pair had a tiny hole from a corkscrew she'd also left in there.

"I must have accidentally taken it from Kris's," she thought, and ran her hand down the leg of the tights to see how big the hole stretched. When her fingers were almost at the hole, it spread and ripped all the way up one leg. She had to toss them and wear the other pair she'd bought, though they were dark gray instead of the black that perfectly matched her skirt.

The very next night, she dreamed she'd remembered to wear the tights, brand new tights with no holes or rips, but that the tattoo somehow broke through, tearing them away so it was exposed yet again. When she woke the next morning, she found her favorite pair of daisy duke's, the ones she had always made the most money in, laid out at the end of the bed. Beside them was a floral lei she'd worn at the last themed party at the bar. What a relief it would be to never work one of those again.

Each night the nightmares grew worse. They were always about her tattoo, and every morning there was something different out around the house, some remnant of her life at the bar: a mask from Halloween, a specialty cup from St. Patrick's Day, even her earplugs from the Battle of the Bands. She thought she was so tired and stressed that she was organizing in her sleep.

By midweek, the tattoo had started to grow in her dreams. At first she'd look down and it would be just a few inches larger, a few shades brighter, and she'd try to cover it with makeup to still be able to hide it under tights. By the end of the week, the tattoo had grown to outrageous proportions, creeping up her leg and onto her thigh like a beanstalk. That weekend, she dreamed the fairy tattoo was as big as ever, but cleverly hidden under a pantsuit. Suddenly, as she and Sandra were talking to a client, her clothes started to rip and bits of the tattoo bulged through like the arms of the Incredible Hulk. Most mornings, Elizabeth could swear she woke to the sound of the fairy giggling in her ears.

Elizabeth began to stay up later to avoid the nightmares, and then she stopped sleeping altogether. She stayed awake organizing. Big piles turned into many smaller ones, but she never seemed to get more than a few items into the appropriate containers. She still couldn't find anything when she needed it. She bought a label maker and soon everything had its own name, color-coordinated with its importance to her. She put post-it notes on everything they would adhere to, reminding her what she had to do next. She never returned personal phone calls, feeling that she couldn't afford to be tempted back into her old life. She had to get it together, and a social life just didn't fit that image at the moment.

"It's all I can do to get to work these days," she admitted to Kris when she dropped by Elizabeth's house unannounced one afternoon.

"You haven't returned a single phone call in three weeks!"

"I'm sorry. It's just that I want to do a good job. It's a lot of pressure."

"Just let me know when you have time for a friend," Kris replied and left.

Elizabeth vowed that as soon as she could get some rest she would see more of Kris. Though she had bags under her eyes and moved at a much slower pace, Elizabeth had been doing well at work. So well Sandra gave the shareholders convention to her to finish up as her first solo project. She settled everything with the client—the ballroom, the caterers, the decorators, and the entertainment, even the bar setup, for which she called in a few favors. Jerry, her old boss/crush of the week from a few years back, was more than happy to lend her some of his best bartenders for beer and wine, and even offered to work the liquor bar himself.

She was excited for the event, but her nerves were beginning to show. The week before the event, she confined herself to her office unless with a client or getting coffee. This meant she was the only witness to the absurd but apparently real-life growth of her ugly tattoo.

The vines took over her body almost to the armpits, and the flower covered half her rear. It really did look like a huge, ill-colored bruise of orange and purple. She couldn't feel it growing, but if she touched it, the skin seemed slightly more raised than before. Bumpier, more *real*. The one-legged fairy herself had somehow changed her shape, but was as ugly and wicked as ever and much larger. Her penciled hair often stood on its ends, and her features made her look like an addict. The wand was tucked like a weapon through her broken wings, and she stood on her one leg in defiance with hands on hips. The figure looked more like a beaten she-warrior than a fairy, standing boldly naked all the way up Elizabeth's thigh. Luckily, the fairy had only peeked out in public a few times, and Elizabeth was able to conceal her before anyone noticed.

Once it was at the coffee machine in the office lounge. Elizabeth had gone in for her third cup of the afternoon and found the secretaries sitting at the little round table in the middle of the room. They looked startled at first, but then the older one with the nice jewelry smiled and asked Elizabeth to join them for a drink after work.

"We're celebrating the end of winter!" the younger one blurted out.

"I'm sorry, but I have a mound of laundry to do tonight," she told them, though she had already done the laundry, cleaned the bathroom, and organized most of the bedroom that week. They nodded, and she poured herself another cup of coffee. Just as the coffee was hitting the bottom of her travel cup, she thought she saw a tiny hand grab the cuff of her pants from the inside and slyly inch up her leg. Then a small, pleading eye peeked out. Elizabeth slapped her ankle as if swatting a mosquito just as Sandra came in.

"Are you all set for the shareholders this weekend, Elizabeth?" she asked.

"I think everything's set." She tried to sound excited, but it came out flat.

"Don't worry, I'm sure it will all work out fine," Sandra said as she left the lounge.

Elizabeth wasn't so sure, but all she really had left to do was the event itself—and to decide what to wear for the event. Panic shot through her.

That night, after sorting her laundry and going through her closet again, she gave up and went shopping. She found a navy pantsuit, and to cover the growing tattoo, she went with a high-collared, dark camisole instead of a white button-down, though it was well out of season. She even bought some dark boots that laced up nice and tight, all the way to her knee—not because they were on sale, though that certainly made them worth it, but as extra insurance. Even though the tattoo had outgrown its spot on her leg, Elizabeth thought if she secured it at the ankle, its original source, this would somehow keep the fairy still and her secret safe.

~ * ~

The night of the event, her stomach flipped as she glanced at her well-covered body. She had pulled on a pair of dark hose, then her pants, and laced up the boots as tightly as she could.

"The thing couldn't possibly move," she thought, "trapped under all these layers."

Though it took her half an hour to find her keys, she finally got out the door and arrived early enough to put the final touches on the table arrangements.

The venue was beautifully dim and impeccably decorated with modern seating and minimalist tables. A jazz band played softly in the background while she and Mr. Wallace greeted guests. There were a few microphone problems during the first speech, but Elizabeth scornfully reprimanded the sound coordinator and no other entertainment bobbles occurred the rest of the evening. As the event was winding down, Elizabeth was mingling with the hobnobbers who represented much of the rich elite in the area when her client approached her.

"Good job, Elizabeth! Here's to not having spoiled seafood!" Mr. Wallace said, and raised his glass of champagne to Elizabeth, who awkwardly held her empty fist up to his glass.

"Where's your drink? Have a glass of champagne," he suggested.

"Oh, no thank you, Mr. Wallace. It might go to my head."

"You haven't had anything all night. You deserve it for working so hard."

"No, thank you. I don't think I should, really," Elizabeth insisted.

"Okay, but you know what they say. All work and no play…"

Elizabeth didn't care that they said. She was exhausted from lack of sleep, the stress, and her cheeks hurt from the perma-grin she felt she had to maintain until the last guest left the building. She was sure a glass of champagne would put her into a sleepwalking stupor, and the thought of more nightmares smeared her smile into a straight stare. A loud crash broke her momentary trance.

One of the portable bars—the biggest, the liquor bar—was tipped on its side and the entire top had been swiped clean. A pile of broken and dripping bottles covered the floor beside it. Jerry, Elizabeth's former boss and the guy she once thought was the cutest and most together dude on the planet, looked pale, sickly, disheveled, and covered in sweat. He just stood there with his mouth wide open, his hands thrown up in the air. A wet rag hung limp from one hand.

Elizabeth thought he must have bumped it in his rush to clean up and go home. "What a slacker," she thought. Long strides took her toward the bar.

"I hope you don't expect reimbursement," she said in a low but firm voice.

A look of hurt flashed across Jerry's face, but then when he tried to explain, he looked confused. "I swear I saw… It wasn't me… But it happened so fast. Someone stumbled into the bar and grabbed the tequila…"

"What? Have you been drinking?" Elizabeth said and stopped.

Horrified at the thought that crossed her mind, she looked down at her right leg and gasped. Her pants were jacked up, her hose torn, and the laces on her new boots broken. How did she not even notice? She ran to the bathroom, hoping for the first time since she got the tattoo that she would find it back on her leg. She rushed through the swinging doors and lifted up the pants leg. No fairy.

She ran into a stall in case someone came in, but left the door open so she could still see the mirror. She took off her boots, slid off her pants and hose. Still no fairy. She struggled out of her jacket and pulled off the camisole. Completely naked, she saw the vines tracing all the way up to her neck, the blue clouds covering half her body, the bruise of a flower still covering her rear—but the fairy was gone. Even her wand was nowhere to be found.

"Shit," she said as she glared at the vines and distorted blue clouds with their missing centerpiece.

There was a groan from the stall directly in front of her. She scrambled back into her clothes and bent to peek under the door. The stall appeared to be empty, but she heard another whimper and knew it had to be the fairy. Her first instinct was to run. Good riddance to the fairy and her crazy imagination. Then she heard it throw up and begin to cry. She slowly opened the stall door, barefoot and holding her jacket.

A strange transparency, flesh but not quite flesh, hung over the toilet. At about three feet tall, its feet dangled. Its pierced wings with the wand through them drooped. Elizabeth softened and put her arm around the fairy. She accidentally pricked herself again with the fairy's wand.

"Ouch, that thing is sharp." She pulled her hand back.

The fairy looked up at her with a clouded gaze. Her hair was knotted and torn, her body bruised. She had a black eye and several cuts on her arms and legs.

"I hope you're happy, *Elizabeth*. Now I'm really ugly!"

"What did I do?" Elizabeth retorted. "Why couldn't you just stay put on my leg, tonight of all nights?" Vowing to herself she would seek therapy first thing on Monday, Elizabeth couldn't help but feel sorry for the sad little creature. "What happened to you, anyway? Are you going to be okay?"

Tears rolled down the fairy's face. "The bar tipped to one side a bit when I decided to climb up and find a bottle that was already open. I almost fell right into the pile of broken bottles before I made it into the bathroom. Everyone was almost gone, and I was just doing what you wanted. I'm you—or, sort of."

The fairy held up her translucent hands, seeming mesmerized by them.

"I would never get this messed up."

"Well, there are lots of things you haven't let yourself do lately, and all that tension has to work itself out somehow. I tend to exaggerate. I'm a fairy, after all," she muttered, just before plunging her face into the toilet to throw up again.

Panic-stricken questions ran through Elizabeth's head. *"Oh, God! What have I not been doing?"*

"Like I said, lots of things." The fairy wiped her mouth with the back of her hand and sat up on the side of the toilet seat.

Elizabeth startled at the reply. She didn't remember asking the question out loud. The fairy sat up straighter, smiling, swaying, and swinging her dangling legs. Elizabeth noticed the fairy was swinging *both* of her legs, and remembered her fairy had only one.

"Wait, how did you get your other leg?"

"It's been tucked under my ass for the past five years!" the fairy said in spite. "By the way, would you mind reconsidering the laser thing, even if you do manage to save enough money? I would hate to lose any body parts for good."

"You sure are demanding for having possibly cost me my job."

"You would be, too, if you had to balance a workaholic after sitting motionless for five years. Besides, I saw that Mr. Wallace earlier—drunk as a skunk. You won't get fired," she said, regaining her color. "If you ever think of getting some touch-ups done to me, I've got a few requests."

"Oh, yeah?" Elizabeth asked as she slid her boots on and zipped them up.

"Clothes would be a good start. A nice leafy halter top with a petal skirt, maybe. And you have got to do something about my wings. These stick things don't even work. Oh, and my hair…"

The fairy continued to ramble as Elizabeth threw her jacket around her and carried her to the car, careful to avoid the prick of the wand again. She promised to do what she could afford for the fairy, so long as she and the rest of the tattoo shrank back to normal size and stayed put on her leg.

Just as she was buckling the fairy in, she spotted Jerry across the lot and quickly shut the car door, hoping her tinted windows would be dark enough.

"Hey, Liz, you okay? I'm really sorry. I have no idea what happened," he said as he got to his car, parked conveniently next to hers. "I didn't touch the liquor, I swear. I must be totally tired and maybe dozed off. Is there anything I can do to make this right?"

"It's Eliz—You know what, it's okay. I'll figure out how to get it taken care of."

"Are you sure?" he said, and unlocked his car—his incredibly clean car, with an organizer in the back. "You know I don't drink on the job."

"I know. I'm sorry I accused you."

"No worries. You'll get it all sorted out. Except for the bar mishap, it was a fantastic party—super classy." He smiled at her, and Elizabeth remembered why she had liked him so much.

Just then, she felt the tattoo calmly shrinking down her body.

~ * ~ * ~

Brandy T. Wilson, PhD, is the author of *The Palace Blues: A Novel,* a 2015 Lambda Literary Award Finalist in Lesbian Fiction and winner of the Alice B. Readers' Lavender Award. Wilson was an Astraea Emerging Lesbian Writers Fund Finalist, a Lambda Literary Retreat Emerging LGBT Voices Fellow in fiction, and a recipient of three Bread Loaf Writers' Conference scholarships. Her work has appeared in Robert Olen Butler's *From Where You Dream, Ninth Letter, G.R.I.T.S. Girls Raised in the South, Pank Magazine, Sinister Wisdom,* and *Lumina* among others.

She is an Associate Professor of English and Creative Writing at the Mississippi University for Women where she teaches fiction writing, LGBTQ literature, and is the faculty advisor for *Ponder Review.* She lives in Memphis with her son, Finn, and their two cats, August and Paris.

Dandelion

Lucy D. Ford

In the Whispertrees Wood, on a moonless night, a dryad unfolded from the trunk of a tall oak tree. Her hair was green as deepest water, flowers and vines were her garb, and luminous eyes looked out from her fresh young face. From the distance, over the horizon, came the echo of a cry. Its loneliness caught deep inside her heart.

Barefoot, she stepped between blooming shrubs at the forest's edge. Branches tossed and creaked in protest.

"Stay, stay!" the leafkin cried. "There's naught beyond the Whispertrees Wood. Naught but the Fargreen Meadows, and death!"

The dryad answered, her voice sweet as song. "Magic calls to me, dearest friends. By leafglow and by starshine, I must go."

So she traveled out from the Whispertrees Wood. The dryad wandered through the Fargreen Meadows until the dawn wove her shadow across the lea. Emerald hair was duller now, and her garb was of seed pods and berries. No more the verdant wood, but wildflowers covered the earth. Bees and butterflies went with her to the Rushling Brook.

There dwelt the gillkin, silver of fin. From the shimmering creek they cried, "Welcome, dear sister, and stay a while. No need to roam farther. Naught lies beyond the Rushling Brook. Naught but the Pricklegrass Hills, and death!"

She paused to cool her feet in the gentle waters, until she heard a whisper soft as windkin feathers. Its sorrow caught her heart and drew her on.

"I thank you, dear gillkin, but magic calls to me. By reedshine and by dawnlight, I must go."

She drank a sweet draught from the Rushling Brook and made her way over the Pricklegrass Hills. The rising sun turned her green hair to golden brown and thinned her fresh young face. Wildflowers gave way to weeds, and her garb was of thistles and thorns.

In the noontime heat, she came to a canyon where once a goodly river flowed. Stony spires loomed over shrinking pools, and a wind moaned between them. Little scalekin, with eyes like ebon beads, skittered among the rocks.

"Welcome, dear sister, and rest beneath our stones," they hissed to her. "No need to roam farther. Naught lies beyond the Crackstone Wash. Naught but the Chokedust Plain, and death!"

The dryad paused in the shade of the stones. She squinted up, up, where the burning sun stung her sunken eyes. Yet the wind held a sigh, soft as a fly's buzzing. Weary as she was, the fear caught her heart and drew her on.

"I thank you, dear scalekin, but magic calls to me. By rockshine and by thorngleam, I must go."

So she climbed over the rocks and ventured forth over the Chokedust Plain. Weeds gave way to sand and her garb was the husks of fallen leaves. Brown hair dried pale as hay, and bright eyes grew dull in her wizened face.

In the evening light she came to a fence of dead wood and wires. Beyond that line, towers of glass and steel reared up high. There the rustkin patrolled with spears of torn metal. Their whisper scratched like thorns.

"Welcome, fair sister, and here you stay. For we guard the Withertines, the grimkin town. They hold no love, nor magic, but cleave to the power of money alone. Turn back!"

The dryad gazed across the Shearwire Fence and shuddered at what she saw. No living thing grew in the Withertines, where all was paved with bitter tar. Plastic boxes raced on rubber wheels. Lights glared from every side and yet showed nothing. Chimneys stretched up and up, belching fumes like earthbound dragons.

Yet a voice trickled between the towers, faint as a flower petal falling. Its desperation seized her heart and drew her on.

"Alas, dear rustkin," the dryad sighed. "Magic calls to me. By coalfire and by arclight, I must go."

"It is death for such as you to enter," the rustkin screeched, and they barred her way.

"One is trapped but not yet dead." Her lucid eyes were ancient and sad. "I will find him, or I deserve my fate."

She bent to climb through the Shearwire Fence. Stinging scratches pierced her skin, mayhap from rustkin blades or mayhap the wicked wires, but the dryad did not turn away. She hobbled forward, though she was withered and bent, garbed in rags. Hard pavement battered her feet. Straw-colored hair turned wispy white, and her face was shriveled as a dried-out plum.

Wonders passed on every side, gleaming offices and shops that blazed with light. Everywhere was noise and stink. Grimkin scurried hither and yon. No one looked twice at a tatty old woman.

She wandered, bewildered, for the forlorn call was drowned in the tide of grimkin greed. Until a door banged open, and a grimkin burst out from a fine, tall house.

"Charwoman!" he bellowed. "You're late!"

The dryad jumped, but as his loud cry faded she heard a quiet sob of despair. She followed the grimkin into his house, and there she saw more marvels: mosaic floors, polished furniture, silver vessels and crystal chandeliers.

"Get to work," yelled the grimkin. "I'm going out, and you'd better be done when I get back!"

She picked up a bucket and broom, and went to sweep the ashes from the fireplace. Once he saw her at work, the grimkin strutted back out. The dryad made her way through the house, from that fireplace to this. Always she listened for the fading cry. It came and went, softer than ever, until she feared the rustkin were right and its hope was lost.

Yet patiently she searched up the stairs and to the back of the house, where a steel-clad door blocked her way.

The dryad was weary, her magic thin as a willow leaf, but she summoned what she had. "Open to me, by marble and midnight."

The door swung free, and she entered a strongroom. Boxes were stacked from ceiling to floor, and to one side an old wooden trunk was half buried by money bags. How any thing of magic could come to such a place, she didn't know. Perhaps this was its only refuge from grimkin greed.

She moved the bags and knelt to whisper, "Open to me, by quicksand and moondark."

The trunk clicked open, and a strongbox rested within. "Open to me, by iron and ashpall."

The lid snapped up. Inside was a bulging satchel. The dryad trembled with weakness, but still she lifted it out. A jumble of fine silks and lace filled the satchel. Buried in the heap was an ivory trinket box. Inside the trinket box was a tangle of gold chains, pendants and pins. One gaudy ring gleamed with a secret fire.

As she plucked it out, a tiny whisper came: "Dear sister, save me!"

She cried, "I will!"

The aged dryad twisted the ring, and the jewel slid aside. There, resting in a hidden chamber, was a single pearl. Before she could open it, a loud bang came from below stairs.

The grimkin had returned! With shaking fingers, she slipped the pearl under her tongue and quickly replaced the jewel, the ring, the trinket box, and the satchel.

Her magic felt thin as a blade of grass, but she summoned what she had. "By iron and ashpall, lock." The metal box shut itself.

"By quicksand and moondark, lock." The wooden trunk sealed tight as a mussel shell.

She heaved a few bags on top of the trunk and shuffled out the door. "By marble and midnight, lock."

Then she took up the broom and bucket of ashes, and hobbled down the stairs. The grimkin was kissing a lady grimkin, but he hollered when he saw the dryad.

"Aren't you done yet? Get out!" And he threw a coin at her.

The dryad scratched after the coin, making her way down with the ashes. All the while, the tiny lump lay beneath her tongue, a secret and a terror. She was sure the grimkin would know what she had taken, but the lady grimkin was stroking his ears. He couldn't wait to shove the dryad out the door.

Alone, the dryad rested on the steps. The night was full of noise and foul fumes. She was weak and wan, tired beyond imagining, but she could not survive in a land without magic.

She left the coin, the bucket and the broom, and stood up straight as she could. "By gravel and gaslight, I come home."

With the pearl still tucked beneath her tongue, she set off through the Withertines. The town confused her, with every glass tower and street sign just like the others, until she thought she was doomed to wander forever.

At last a fresh breeze touched her sunken cheek. She followed it, footsore and filthy, until she saw the dull glint of the Shearwire Fence on the other side of a hot, black highway.

The rustkin pointed their jagged spears at her. "Go back! No creature of smoke and ash shall leave the Grimkin town! Go back!"

Again the dryad stooped to pass the Shearwire Fence, and again rustkin spears pricked at her. But the moment her foot touched the earth—even on the Chokedust Plain—a sliver of her strength returned.

Tenderly the dryad spat the pearl into her palm. "Dear rustkin, behold! I have brought forth what was lost in that poisoned place. I shall bear it away to the Whispertrees Wood, where it may flourish."

The dryad squeezed the pearl, and a tiny crack split its gleaming face. From inside she picked out a single seed. Her magic felt thin as a hair, yet she breathed all she had upon the seed.

At once the seed case popped open. Out sprang a wee green sprout. The rustkin creaked a sigh of wonder. "Well done, brave sister."

The dryad turned her face to the east, toward her home. It was a very long way, but she stepped forth all the same.

"Farewell, dear rustkin. By coalfire and by arclight, I go home."

She walked and walked, over gravel and dust. Slowly her rags became bark and her white hair grew yellow as straw. All the while the little sprout grew roots to tickle her palm.

On the edge of dawn she came to the Crackstone Wash, where scalekin stirred in crannies of rock. They whispered, "Well done, kind sister."

She answered, "Farewell, dear scalekin. By rockshine and by thornlight, I go home."

The dryad crossed the dry river and entered the hills, where weeds swayed in the morning light. Their fragrance brought strength to her limbs and banished her wrinkles. No longer a crone, she strode the Pricklegrass Hills with brown hair flowing.

The seedling, too, grew in life and power. Spreading roots trickled between her fingers. Leaves stretched long and narrow. Above them the green knob of a bud bobbed and bowed. As the sun rose higher, the bud swelled and opened as a yellow tuft.

The gillkin in the Rushling Brook squealed with delight. "Well done, fair sister!"

She laughed for joy and called to them, "Farewell, dear gillkin. By reedshine and by dawnlight, I go home!"

The dryad skipped and twirled as she crossed the Fargreen Meadows. Wildflowers gave way to flowering shrubs, and once more she was clad in seed pods and berries. Bees swarmed to kiss the flower in her hand, until it joyfully closed its eyes. As the sun shone down, it opened again in a puff white as the clouds above.

The dryad called out, "Aid us, dear windkin!"

The windkin came, dancing and swirling sheer robes of air. They teased the flower and caught each delicate tuft, until the multitude of new seeds drifted across the land. Some alit in the Fargreen Meadows or grew beside the Rushling Brook. Some flew back to the Crackstone Wash. One or two even came to earth along the Shearwire Fence and cheered the hearts of the proud Rustkin.

But many of the seeds caught in her emerald hair or on her robe of flowers and vines, and straightway burst into sprouts. So the dryad returned to the Whispertrees Wood crowned with gold, her robe ermined by white puffs.

Leafkin swarmed to meet her. "Welcome, dear sister, and welcome home!"

The dryad said, "I have followed my heart and brought forth magic from the barren Withertines. For magic cannot be kept inside a ring or a box. It cannot be bound in a chest or a trunk. Magic belongs to everyone, and see! By leafglow and by starshine, I have brought it home."

The dryad gazed back across the realms she had traveled. Everywhere bright flowers bloomed, and silvery puffs floated in the golden dusk. With them their magic, so long trapped, burst forth upon the land.

She slipped back into the Whispertrees Wood to rest, contented.

~ * ~ * ~

Lucy D. Ford is the pen name of fantasy author Deby Fredericks. She has sold children's poetry and short stories to *Boys Life, Ladybug, Babybug, Cricket*, and other print magazines. Her novel for middle grades, *Masters of Air & Fire*, appeared from Sky Warrior Books in 2012 and was reissued in 2023. Her short story collection, *Aunt Ursula's Atlas*, released in 2016.

Find out more at her web site, www.debyfredericks.com, or her blog, Wyrmflight.wordpress.com.

More Great Anthologies from WolfSinger Publications

Borne in the Blood – edited by Carol Hightshoe

Delve into the mysterious and powerful world of blood.

This collection of enthralling stories explores the multifaceted essence of blood—as a symbol of life, a medium of magic, and a bond of kinship. From the chilling tale of a minstrel haunted by a spectral king to the whimsical account of a vampire ice cream vendor, each story weaves a unique narrative around the theme of blood. Encounter a woman whose body bizarrely intertwines with metallic elements, and follow a girl's journey as she confronts her isolation due to her heritage. Feel chills as those who were wronged reach across the years to have their final revenge on the blood descendants of those who oppressed them.

Shifters, Vampires, Witches, and other ordinary and extraordinary folk—all bound together by that which they carry in their blood.

These tales will transport you through a spectrum of emotions, from the depths of fear to the heights of fantasy, as you unravel the mysteries and power that lie within the blood.

Proceeds from sales of Borne in the Blood will be donated to the Multiple Myeloma Research Foundation – themmrf.org/

Space Brides – edited by Dana Bell

Tired of those lonely dark nights? No one in your settlement suitable? We are here to help! We will help you find the bride or husband to keep you company, raise your children, and be your partner building a dream together. Contact us directly and give us your specifications. Success guaranteed.

In this collection of 15 testimonials read about the challenges and triumphs of some of our clients as they found love on the frontier of space.

From aliens to vampires, we brought these couples together and together they found acceptance and love—each in their own way.

A man with three kids finds an unexpected match in the brother of the woman he had contracted to marry when she runs away.

A woman running away from an abusive marriage finds acceptance and respect with a colony group that marries everyone to everyone in order to ensure they know they belong to a family.

A woman constantly rejected because of her skin color and origins finds acceptance and love with a wounded soldier.

Even though we encourage absolute honesty in your profile and correspondence with your potential spouse—many people don't. However, like some of the testimonials you'll read here; they still manage to expand their horizons—together.

Contact or walk into any of our offices 24/7. We are here to help you find that special someone and start a new future!

Other conditions apply.
Please ask for more information before contract is drawn up and signed.

The Dragon's Hoard — edited by Carol Hightshoe

Dragons are well known for their hoards—but not all hoards are created equal.

A young dragon starts his hoard with some very precious gifts.

One dragon shares her complaints about taxes with a friend as they wait for a lunch delivery.

Another dragon defends her most precious treasures against a group of greedy goblins.

And yet another may hold the solution to saving the Earth after a devastating apocalypse in his collection of bottled treasures.

In addition to the normal gold, silver and jewels here you will find dragons who collect many different treasures. 25 storytellers invite you to enter The Dragon's Hoard and share the treasures within.

Tails From the Front Lines 2 — edited by Carol Hightshoe

Come meet some of the four-legged members of Law Enforcement who also serve and protect.

Here our authors will introduce you to the brave K9 officers who serve alongside their human partners. They are their eyes, ears, noses and sometimes when necessary they are their shield, protecting others.

Proceeds from this anthology will be donated to the El Paso County (Colorado) Sheriff's Office K9 program in memory of K9 Jinx who was killed in the line of duty on April 11, 2022.

Ring of Fire — edited by Dana Bell

Enter the Ring of Fire, as unpredictable as the land masses shaking a city and volcanoes erupting covering the landscape. Could there be other reasons for these events? Or could these rings be more than a geological location.

They may be dragons playing tricks
or magic portals opened to mysterious realms
or sacrificing the best work of a lifetime.
Perhaps a rescue during a forest fire
or an attempt to raise the dead
or even while attending a high school reunion.

Journeys are taken to far off lands, another world, and through caves, each with their own unique twist.

Each tale presents a new idea on what the Ring of Fire could be. It is more than what many have been led to believe. Pull up a chair and warm yourself by our fires—just don't let yourself get burned.

Out of the Darkness — edited by Carol Hightshoe

Mental Health issues have long been stigmatized, with those facing them pushed into the shadows, often unable to deal with the darkness they find themselves trapped in.

In this collection, stories explore many types of darkness—Suicidal Ideation, Death from Suicide, Survivor's Guilt, PTSD, Chronic Pain, Chronic Illness, Depression, Death of a Loved One, Secrets, Bullying, and other forms of darkness are explored. Some related to mental health issues and some not, but all of them offer very human perspectives. As in real life, some stories have happy endings and sadly others don't.

We offer these stories of darkness without judgement, but with hope and compassion. Some roads should never have to be traveled —but we understand that for many they are being traveled alone.

Proceeds from sales of Out of the Darkness will be donated to the American Foundation for Suicide Prevention—for more information on AFSP please visit their website at: afsp.org.

For those who may be in crisis—PLEASE call or text 988 to connect directly to the 988 Suicide and Crisis Lifeline. For those outside the US please connect with your local lifeline

Never Cheat a Witch – edited by Carol Hightshoe

Magical curses. Arcane revenge. Being transformed into a frog. Things evil witches do to mere mortals who cross their path. But, what if there is more to the story...

Deals made with a witch are magically binding and can bring dire consequences to those who even think about breaking them.

Whether they are seeking revenge for wrongs done to them, helping others or simply trying to live their lives—it is NEVER wise to try and cheat a witch.

Open your spell book and join our authors as they relate tales of witches and mortals. From classic fantasy witches to modern day witches and even the legendary Baba Yaga. Good and Evil as well as every shade of gray in between. And, yes—there is a prince who is turned into a frog.

Time Capsules – edited by Carol Hightshoe

Time Capsules–history and mystery–a gift or a message from the past to the future. Messages that can easily be misunderstood.

What were the reasons for passing along a pair of pink, fuzzy handcuffs?

A glass vial containing a perfect dandelion puff?

A Japanese Katana?

A red and blue scarf?

A wooden spoon?

What magic do these items contain? What stories do they tell?

From the past to the future. Mysteries and meanings abound within these pages, as well as reminders of the things people find precious. What will you find?

US/THEM – edited by Carol Hightshoe

Fear of the *Other* breeds hatred of the *Other*

They aren't like us—so they must be bad...inferior... dangerous...

Humans are by nature social animals, but we tend to bond with other humans with whom we have something in common: beliefs, experiences, likes and dislikes, etc.

With the expansion of humans across the planet, it seems that, even as our numbers grow, we find ways to whittle our groups into ever narrower, specialized, and exclusive blocks. We target the *Other* for the most minor differences and interpret everything from *THEM* as an insult or an attack.

Within these pages you will witness hatred, intolerance and fanaticism as well as love, understanding and acceptance. Most of all, I, and the authors, hope you discover stories that will cause you to pause and think before condemning someone as being *THEM* and not *US*.

Crunchy with Ketchup – edited by Carol Hightshoe

It has been said that one should never meddle in the affairs of dragons—for you are crunchy and taste good with ketchup.

Come enter the dragon's lair.

Take your chances with other would-be heroes and heroines who decide to face off against one of the biggest, baddest predators ever.

Witness a dragon civil war.

Hear the true story of the Battle of New Orleans.

Find out what it's like in the belly of a dragon.

Discover why cats can spell disaster when stealing a dragon's egg.

Meet a group of dragon riders who protect us from nuclear devastation.

Follow legends of modern dragons, only to find something very unexpected.

And more...

Crunchy with Chocolate – edited by Carol Hightshoe

It has been said that one should never meddle in the affairs of dragons—for you are crunchy and taste good with chocolate.

Come enter the dragon's lair and roll the dice. Within these pages you will still meet some of the biggest, baddest predators ever—but if you are lucky, you will also discover some that have a sweeter side.

Meet a dragon with a soft spot for hard luck cases and another who is a hopeless romantic.

Enjoy a musical battle between a dragon and the specter of one of the greatest guitarists to ever play.

Meet a dragon in trouble with other magical creatures because he enjoys hanging out with human children.

Join a mother and daughter and their teams of dragons on a dangerous cross-country race.

Reconnect with an imaginary friend—who is not so imaginary and escape the isolation of the pandemic.

And more…

So enter in BUT tread carefully—remember you are crunchy and taste good with chocolate.

Visit us at wolfsingerpubs.com

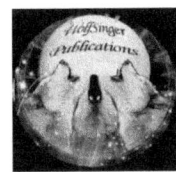